G000153538

KARMA IS A BITCH

KARMA IS A BITCH

THE UNBELIEVABLE MR. BROWNSTONE™ BOOK TWELVE

MICHAEL ANDERLE

DISRUPTIVE IMAGINATION®

THE KARMA IS A BITCH TEAM

Special Thanks
to Mike Ross
for BBQ Consulting
Jessie Rae's BBQ - Las Vegas, NV

Thanks to the JIT Readers

James Caplan
Misty Roa
Kelly O'Donnell
John Ashmore
Danika Fedeli
Angel LaVey
Nicole Emens
Peter Manis
Keith Verret
Larry Omans
Daniel Weigert
Micky Cocker
Paul Westman

If I've missed anyone, please let me know!

Editor
Lynne Stiegler

*To Family, Friends and
Those Who Love
to Read.
May We All Enjoy Grace
to Live the Life We Are
Called.*

CHAPTER ONE

The chaos entity who went by He Who Hunts floated in a darkened chamber surrounded by glowing windows in the air, each a magical screen relaying images and sensations from the Brownstone team's assault on the Council base. He watched as summoned monsters and wizards fell to bullets, grenades, rockets, and even swords.

The sight of so much death and havoc filled him with something humans might refer to as joy. Maybe satisfaction.

The foolish government wizards and witches of the Paranormal Defense Agency believed they had shielded the entire facility, but his magic could pierce their feeble attempts. He was beyond them. He was beyond even the other members of the Council. Even so, scrying into the past was draining him, but it was useful to evaluate the people who had defeated his allies.

In truth, He Who Hunts could have drawn off the dark power of other dimensions to open a portal and reinforce the Council as Brownstone and his allies slaughtered them, but he didn't care. The Council had served its purpose. He had used them to gather the key artifacts needed to pierce reality and delve deeper into darker and more chaotic realms. With a few more years of effort, he'd be able to connect them directly to Earth and Oriceran. A wonderful age would await.

Earth would come first. Understanding of magic remained shallower in the Earth nations and societies. His plan could proceed before they could reverse it. Once Earth fell, repeating the process on Oriceran would be trivial despite their greater capability for sorcery.

He Who Hunts flicked a tendril of red mist against one of the magical screens, which shimmered and changed. An armored Brownstone battled soul-drinkers, the battle ending with the bounty hunter blasting green beams that blew holes through the monsters with ease.

The limitations of his scrying magic summoned the first few sparks of frustration in He Who Hunts. When the Council had checked into Brownstone, they'd heard little of him using abilities such as the ones displayed in these images, which meant the bounty hunter had been holding back for some reason. The reasons for that would be critical to evaluating how to deal with the man.

Considering the level of injury and death the Council had wreaked upon the military and other bounty hunters, Brownstone would probably have thought it necessary to use his true abilities. If anything, it made less sense for him to do that given that he'd brought along so many weaker men than himself. Even if they had been well-equipped and trained, they'd been seriously injured. One of his men had even been killed.

No. Brownstone wouldn't hold back out of contempt for the Council's power. Something else had to be motivating him.

Fear. That was the most likely explanation. Brownstone feared his true abilities, which meant they relied on a source he couldn't control or they required a cost he didn't want to pay. There were countless types of dangerous and yet powerful magics that could be behind the bounty hunter's power.

He Who Hunts didn't care about the source. He only cared about gaining a new and powerful tool.

The magical screens vanished and He Who Hunts floated toward the door, passing over piles of dead bodies lying on the ground. Most lacked their heads, and their bodies were withered and cracked. Several had holes in their hearts surrounded by blackened flesh. All had fed him.

The creature glided over to a small glass case, and with a flick of his mist tendril, the lid flipped open. A glowing red crystal lay inside, one of the few artifacts that had survived the attention of both the government forces and Brownstone. Most of the other artifacts he'd already fed on, using their energy to strengthen himself even at the cost of their destruction.

The losses weren't important. His goals only required his growing strength, not ephemeral connections to weak mortals who lacked any true power. The situation was far different from his first few weak years in this dimension.

The crystal presented a rare and useful opportunity; a

tool he could use for the complete corruption of James Brownstone. He Who Hunts would only be able to use the crystal once, but when he controlled the other man, he'd be worth armies of the pathetic wizards and Zain fodder. Unleashing Brownstone upon an unsuspecting city would be glorious to behold.

Such death. Such panic. Such chaos.

He Who Hunts glowed brightly for a few seconds at the thought.

A fool destroyed his powerful enemies. An intelligent creature turned his enemies to his own use and made a mockery of them. Whatever fear Brownstone felt that kept him from always using his true power could be exploited by the red crystal. The man would become a tool to spread chaos and weaken the feeble walls that protected the pathetic dimension holding Earth and Oriceran.

Even so many weeks after the incident, He Who Hunts' spell could sense the rage and anger spilling from Brownstone as he finished off his enemies. The strange armor he wore didn't taste like any magic He Who Hunts knew, but it was clear that negative emotions were critical to its use. That would make the bounty hunter vulnerable to the power of the red crystal. Vulnerable to corruption.

Brownstone had even done He Who Hunts a favor by extinguishing the Council. Their goals had been myopic. Control? Influence? What a laughable notion. There was no true control, only chaos waiting for its chance.

There was a light knock on the door.

"Enter," He Who Hunts hissed in his raspy voice. Every word of normal speech pained him, but some things were necessary to work with lesser beings.

A dozen robed wizards filed into the room. The Council had few forces left, but they could be of use.

One of the wizards bowed over an arm. "We've come as summoned, Master."

He Who Hunts floated over toward the man. He didn't bother with a robe, appearing to them to be nothing more than a swirling mass of red mist and glowing red eyes. Tendrils appeared and disappeared as needed.

"The governments of many nations and their allies have wounded the Council." He Who Hunts floated upward. "Some who claimed loyalty to our great cause have fled. I ask you, are you loyal?"

The wizard stood upright. "We're all loyal. We will not abandon the Council. We'll hunt others if you ask it of us, Master."

The other wizards nodded their agreement.

"Are you willing to sacrifice for the Council?" He Who Hunts asked.

"Yes, Master."

He Who Hunts glided until he was mere inches from the man, the scorching heat of his mist making the man twitch. "What would you sacrifice?"

"E-everything, master."

He Who Hunts floated back, several tendrils growing from his body. "A good final answer."

"Final answer?"

The door slammed shut behind the wizards. They all exchanged glances, fear appearing on their faces.

He Who Hunts rose toward the ceiling, his tendrils floating and twitching. A burning scarlet mist condensed from the air. The lids of four boxes positioned in the cardinal directions within the room blew off, more mist flowing out from the remnants of the artifacts inside.

The wizards turned and rushed for the closed door. The first few to reach it pounded on it.

The mist thickened and the wizards fell to the ground, screaming and clawing at their ears and mouths. Their bodies twisted and contorted. Living gray stone spread over one man. Another grew more legs and a dark carapace.

Each mutation was distinct in its own way. One wizard screamed as half his body tore away and regenerated seconds later, leaving two full men where one had once been. Then four. Then eight.

He Who Hunts surveyed the monsters below him as the screaming continued. He'd changed them and would rule their hearts and minds. Their lives would be limited to weeks, but it didn't matter. They only needed to live long enough to execute his current plan to capture his true target.

"You will be the key, Brownstone," he hissed. "You will become mine. You will unlock chaos."

Motherfucker!

Trey ducked as a bullet shattered the window he'd been looking through. That was what he got for taking on the targets in their home. There was just something about Vegas bounties in houses. They went south more often than in LA. Maybe it was just that he and the rest of the guys didn't know Vegas as well as their home city.

Damn, that was close.

"Motherfucker," he shouted, "it should be a crime to damage a face as handsome as this one."

Lachlan snorted and reloaded his pistol. "I swear every time we go after twins, they be way fucking harder than normal bounties. You think there is some magic shit to being a twin?" He spun and unloaded several rounds through the wall before jumping away.

"I don't really give a fuck." Trey pulled out a flashbang. The criminals had shot out the window, which meant he could now give them a little present. "Just need to distract these fuckers long enough for Max and Isaiah to surprise their asses." He gritted his teeth. "Give me some cover on three, two, one…"

Lachlan fired through the wall again and rolled out of the way to avoid the rifle bullets ripping through it from the opposite direction.

Trey took his chance and hurled the flashbang through the shattered remains of the window. A pop and flash preceded the loud groans of the twin brothers inside, both level threes. A few seconds later the front door crashed open, a victim of Isaiah's foot.

Lachlan shot up to aim through the window. Trey followed suit.

Isaiah and Max tackled the men inside, knocking the criminals and their guns to the floor.

"Stay here," Trey shouted to Lachlan as he sprinted around the corner.

By the time he'd run around the house and into the front room, Max and Isaiah already had the bounties zip-tied and face-down.

"Good job." Trey marched over to the bounties and shook his head. "You're lucky we're the Brownstone Agency, so we ain't gonna beat your asses despite you trying to kill us."

A soft feminine chuckle came from the front door.

Trey spun, his weapon up. A beautiful pale redhead in an Armani suit stood right outside the house, a thin golden wand hanging loosely from her hand.

Victoria Stone. It'd been a while since he'd last run into the witch.

Isaiah and Max brought up their guns, but Trey waved them off as he holstered his weapon.

"It's cool. She ain't here to save these motherfuckers."

Victoria grinned. "How can you be so sure?"

Trey grinned back. "Because you already would have fried our asses, and I doubt you're wasting time working for dumbass motherfuckers like these two bitches."

She laughed. "That's accurate enough. I actually came to grab them, but you damn Brownstone boys are just too fast."

Trey frowned. "Grab them? What? You a cop now?"

Victoria shook her head. "I decided to take up bounty hunting." She holstered her wand inside her jacket and started walking away. "See you."

Trey turned and nodded to Max. "You get them boys ready. I'll be right back." He jogged after the witch.

Lachlan turned the corner and eyed her with confusion but continued into the house without saying anything.

Victoria leaned against the side of the house, arms crossed and lips pursed, which highlighted her bright red lipstick.

Trey gestured toward the front door. "We aren't gonna have a problem, are we? We grabbed those boys fair and square."

She shook her head. "No, I have no interest in poaching your captures."

"I haven't even heard that you were in the hunt scene, and we try to keep an ear to the ground."

Victoria shrugged. "I've been out of town. After that incident with Johns I thought it might be better to avoid Vegas for a while, but it's my home, so I decided to come back." She looked Trey up and down with a slight frown and pointed to an anti-magic deflector hanging around his neck. "Why bring something like that for two common hitmen?"

Trey snorted. "You shitting me? Johns was only a level three, and he had this hot-ass witch guarding him." He smirked. "You never know what you're gonna run into on a bounty hunt, so we like to be more careful nowadays."

Victoria chuckled. "Awfully expensive way to be careful." She shrugged and pushed off the wall. "You're certainly still looking good. Maybe a little bit more muscular than last time."

"That's probably just the bulletproof vest."

She laughed. "Just saying... I'm a woman who knows what she wants, and I think it was a mistake that I didn't connect with you after our last run-in. You seem like a very capable and interesting man."

What the fuck? Am I like catnip to witches?

Trey sighed and rubbed the back of his neck. "Now, straight-up, Victoria, you're fucking fine. No man could deny that, but..."

Victoria arched an eyebrow. "But?"

"I'm kind of seeing someone right now, and I'm a one-witch kind of man."

The corners of Victoria's mouth turned up in a smile. "She's a witch?"

Trey nodded. "Yeah. Potions witch."

Shit. Do I even really have anything with Zoe? I mean, we slept together, but she ain't been wanting to see me much the last couple of weeks, always saying she's busy.

Maybe Zoe ain't want nothing more than she got.

Trey wanted to tell himself he was the same, but that would be a lie, and he knew it. He couldn't get the potions witch out of his mind, even if he had a beautiful witch standing right in front of him asking him out.

Victoria smiled. "I'm not surprised. You're brave and handsome, and there's a certain…quality about you."

"Quality?"

"I don't know. Just call it witch's intuition. I think you'll only grow to be a more impressive man." She shrugged. "Something different than your other friend I ran into that day." She nodded toward the house. "I didn't see him in there. He in LA right now?"

Trey sighed and looked down. "Did you hear at all about how the Brownstone Agency went after the Council?"

Victoria nodded, her smile fading. "Yes, it's not exactly a big secret."

He shrugged. "Shorty got killed by some fuckers working for the Council."

"My condolences." The witch sighed. "I hope it was a good death."

Trey nodded. "He died saving my life. Don't know if that shit is good."

"It's always good to save someone else with your last breath." She locked eyes with him. "I'd encourage you to live up to that sacrifice."

"I try to every day."

Victoria sighed and turned. "I should get going. If I'm not going to get the bounty for the level threes, there are a few easy pick-ups I can manage while you're distracted taking those guys in." She waved. "See you around, Trey."

He waved back and headed into the house again. Victoria was right. The only thing he could do for Shorty now was make sure he'd died for a good man.

I'm gonna keep trying, brother. We at least took out those Council bastards for you, but I'm not gonna forget, not for one minute of one day, what you did for me, Shorty.

CHAPTER TWO

The SUV rumbled through the Mexican scrubland. James grunted. He needed to stop coming down to Mexico only when he had a bounty. He wasn't much for vacations, but it might be nice to hang out in the country when he wasn't going to have to beat or kill someone.

Shit. If it weren't for Jesse Rae's, Vegas might be like that for me, too.

Shay glanced at him from the passenger seat. "Problem?"

James shook his head. "Nah, just thinking that every time I travel, it's like one day of relaxing and food and several days of ass-kicking."

Shay laughed. "Oh. What, you want to take some time off?

He shrugged. "It's not like that. Just getting a little fucking tired of always seeing the worst a place has to offer."

"Getting thoughtful in your old age, huh?" Shay grinned.

James grunted again and shrugged. "Not feeling bad about kicking Council ass, even if it's just leftover foot soldiers."

Shay nodded. "I'm surprised they didn't just send special forces to finish these guys off."

"Senator Johnston said that since the Council cell was in Baja, he preferred for us to handle it."

"Fine by me." Shay smiled. "For me at least, it's relaxing coming to Mexico ever since we destroyed the cartel."

James chuckled, but then his mirth faded. "I got to be honest."

She glanced his way. "What are you talking about?"

"The senator actually asked if I wanted to go with a group of soldiers." James frowned. "I turned him down."

Shay nodded. "No reason to give up money. I'm sure they would have taken some of the reward."

"That's not the reason."

"What, then?"

James' grip tightened around the wheel, and it creaked under the pressure. "Those Council douchebags have made me lose control a few times. Fuck, you've seen it." He shook his head, his brow knitting in concern. "What happens if I lose control and end up hurting a soldier?"

Shay shrugged. "Don't think it's gonna happen."

He glanced her way. "How can you be so sure?"

"Because, yeah, I've seen you lose control, but you were already working with other people. Even if last time you ran off by yourself, you've gone into top-level ass-kicking mode when I was around you, and the AET."

James snorted. "You haven't seen shit."

Shay arched a brow. "What the fuck does that mean?"

"It's not just the armor and the blade anymore. When I totally lose it, Whispy Doom calls it extended advanced transformation. Not just the full suit and the helmet you saw, but some sort of energy blasts."

A light chuckle escaped Shay's lips. "I was wondering what the hell happened to those weird monsters in the vehicle bay. I ended up there when I was trying to chase you down, and I couldn't quite figure out how you blew holes through them with the gear you had." She raised a shoulder. "I don't see the big deal. It's nice to have a few surprises in your back pocket in case you run into someone tougher than you expected."

James shook his head, taking a moment to check his mirrors. Nothing but dust and rocks on the pathetic path passing for a road. "But the only way I get to advanced or extended advanced mode is by being pissed off. Anger. Hatred. That shit." He patted his chest, where the unbonded amulet lay underneath his shirt. "And he fucking gets off on it like an eighteen-year-old at his first strip club."

Shay snorted. "So?"

"So? You don't think that's a bad thing?"

"You worried Yoda's gonna show up and criticize you for going over to the Dark Side or some shit?" Shay rolled her eyes. "This is what you do—you kick ass. Sometimes you get mad and kick more ass. I don't think there's anything wrong with being pissed off when you kick ass. Shit, it's not exactly like I'm always calm when I'm killing people."

James glanced her way, looking for some sign of deception in her face, but she seemed more annoyed than anything. "But I keep getting more powerful. What if I hurt someone who doesn't have it coming?"

"As long as everyone knows the deal, we can manage that. It's not like the military doesn't use big-ass bombs just because they're big-ass bombs. They just make sure none of the friendly guys are near them when they go off."

He grunted. "So now I'm a big-ass bomb?"

Shay laughed. "Basically. Or maybe a Berserker, like in the Norse sagas."

James' mouth twitched. "I've read about them. They were famous for not being able to tell their friends from their enemies."

"Which was why they sent them where their own guys wouldn't be." Shay shook her head. "Look, you're really overthinking this, and you're ignoring the basic fucking reality of us living in a dangerous world. You know the best way to achieve peace?"

He shrugged. "Everyone shares barbeque?"

Shay burst out laughing. "Hell, no. Peace through superior firepower. You're not just a big-ass bomb. You're a nuke, and if we can force peace by nuking some assholes, so be it. Eventually, if they show up with a nuke of their own, maybe we can all agree on something. Until then, keep on doing what you do. Kick ass and take names."

James snorted. "Now I'm a fucking nuke. For all I know, someday some asshole from my home planet will show up to arrest me for using this suit illegally according to galactic law or some shit."

Shay's smile faded, and she sighed. "About that…"

His gaze flicked her way. "You find out something new?"

She shook her head. "I'm kind of at a dead end. The government guys looking into this thing—you know Projects Ragnarok and Nephilim—might know more, but not that Peyton's been able to find, and I've been scouring my library and other resources and hitting only more dead ends. Barely been able to translate any more of the symbols." She shrugged. "I'm honestly unsure if we'll be able to actually track down where you're from unless I stumble across some random alien birth certificate. Maybe some of the shit Peyton's girlfriend is involved in might pay off, but I doubt they'll be releasing anything to the general public. She's pretty clueless about what he knows, from what he's told me."

James grunted. "Big fucking deal."

"Big fucking deal?"

He nodded. "I might have been born on some planet out there, but I grew up on Earth. My people are on Earth and in America. Everyone I give a shit about lives on Earth." He shook his head. "It's not about where you're born. It's about how you choose to live your life, and where you choose to call home. I doubt I'll ever meet some fucker from my home planet, but I don't care."

A soft smile appeared on Shay's face. "Good, I was worried there for a second."

"Worried?"

She nodded. "I have to go on that tomb raid with Lily soon, and I didn't want to leave you if you were going to be all mopey and shit."

James snorted. "I'm never mopey and shit."

Shay snickered. "'Mopey and shit' is like your default setting." She winked. "But I make all that go away." She pointed to the GPS readout on the front console screen. "Looks like we're already there. Let's finish off these assholes and go back to the hotel where I can make sure you're extra non-mopey...even if I'm gonna end up a little sore."

James grinned. "Little motivation never hurt."

Time to go all nuclear.

They parked several hundred yards away from the unassuming adobe house at the end of the road. Split-wood fencing sectioned off dried and cracked ground supporting only a few plants here and there. Someone might have once tried to raise some cattle there, only to find out they'd made a horrible mistake.

Shay stepped out of the SUV. James followed a few seconds later.

"Bond with Whispy Doom," Shay called.

James grunted. "I don't need him for this shit. These guys would barely be threes if they weren't with the Council."

Shay shook her head. "If you're so worried about that thing, you need to use it more, not less. Make sure it knows who's in charge." Shay checked the magazine in her 9mm. "I've had plenty of unstable artifacts that aren't half as useful."

Yeah, guess she's right. He's gonna be an annoying bitch though. Getting mouthier every day.

James nodded and reached under his shirt to yank off the metal separator keeping the amulet from touching his skin. A second later, he hissed as pain shot from his chest, the amulet sinking into his flesh.

Initiation, the amulet sent into his mind.

Naptime is over, James thought back. *Time to do what we do best.*

Kill the enemy. Adapt. Grow stronger.

James grunted. *Yeah, that about sums it up.* He jogged toward the ranch house.

Shay hurried after him. "I thought we were going to hit them with a few drones first. That was what you told me earlier."

"Fuck it. You wanted me to use the damned amulet, I'm using the damned amulet." James pulled out his .45. "We've fought enough of these Council pieces of shit that Whispy Doom's adapted to most anything they've got."

Find stronger enemies. Kill, adapt, and grow stronger for maximum potential. Extended advanced mode is not maximum potential.

Yeah, yeah. I'll just keep getting pissier until I blow up a city. I get it. That would make you happy, wouldn't it, you fucking sadist?

Kill stronger enemies for maximum potential. Environment irrelevant.

James snorted. Every time he used the amulet he understood it more, or maybe Whispy Doom was figuring out how to communicate with him more clearly. He'd had the damned thing his entire life, and it unnerved him to think about what it might have been saying all those years.

Someone threw open the front door of the ranch house, and two men with wands filed out.

James slowed his jog, Shay right behind.

"I'm James Brownstone. I'm working a continuing class-six organizational bounty on the Council, dead or alive. You assholes can surrender right now and take a nice trip, or you can fucking die right here. I don't really give a shit what you choose. I get paid either way."

One of the wizards snorted. "The Council lives. He Who Hunts lives."

James let out a low growl. He hated it when assholes were right.

Find stronger enemy. Engage stronger enemy for advanced adaptation potential.

"Yeah, your last big tough guy from the Council? It's been a few weeks now, and I haven't seen him at any place I've raided, nor any of the military guys." James chuckled. "Sounds like a pussy who doesn't want to fight. And that's assuming he didn't crawl off to bleed to death somewhere."

Shay edged toward a small outhouse for cover. More wizards stepped out of the house until ten men stood there. That was far more than the five James had been told would be present.

Guess it's a two-for-one bounty today.

James shook his head. "Last chance—"

A blindingly white ball of blue-white fire blasted from one of the wands, but James stood firm. The blast crashed into him, the flames burning through his shabby gray coat in an instant. The smell of burnt polyester and cotton filled his nostrils. Other than a slight sting and redness on his chest, no one would even know he'd been hit by a magical fireball.

The wizards' eyes widened and they all spread out, bringing up their wands. They held their breaths, aiming at him, but none daring to break away in a run or say anything else.

Find stronger enemies, Whispy demanded. *Adaptation near maximum for existing attacks. Inefficient use of time.*

I get paid for this shit.

Shay moved in the corner of James' eye. She flattened herself against the outhouse. She'd holstered her pistol and pulled out an adamantine knife.

Good plan. With so many wizards, they're gonna have shielding magic.

James holstered his pistol and yanked out the adamantine knife Shay had lent him.

Need to get my own magic blade. Can't always borrow Shay's shit.

Additional external weapons unnecessary, Whispy Doom sent. *Generate sufficient power for advanced mode or extended advanced mode.*

James snickered. Apparently, his amulet was jealous.

I don't need advanced mode for these assholes. That's like sending a Superbowl team after some AA high school team. Where's the fun in that? Only using you because Shay insisted, otherwise you'd be still asleep.

Female human has maximized tactical possibilities with suggestion.

James snorted. The last thing he needed was Whispy Doom, Alison, and Shay ganging up on him. Maybe he'd been wrong, and Whispy was female. Just what he needed, a woman who could get directly into his head.

Fuck. Need to concentrate. Shut your mo...shut up.

James pointed his knife at the pack of wizards. "That all you got? I fucking personally killed members of the Council, assholes. You really think your weak-ass magic would work on me? Should have taken me up on my surrender offer."

He charged straight toward them. A rainbow of death blasted toward him. Fire. Ice. Electricity. Acid.

Now what the fuck is that purple shit?

Adaptation near maximum for existing attack.

I get that it doesn't hurt much, but... You know what? Forget it.

He grunted as the magic struck him, shredding his jacket, shirt, and pants but accomplishing little more than inflicting a few minor burns and cuts. He continued charging straight at the wizards as they tried to rain death down on him. The only obstacle at this point was the thick and blinding cloud of dust thrown up by all the explosions.

Don't need to see to stab, assholes.

A second later, his theory became reality as his knife pierced the heart of a wizard. The man screamed, and James yanked the blade out. He spun toward the nearest shadow and slashed at the neck. The half-decapitated man fell to the ground gurgling, his blood spraying all over his killer and the ground. Two other screams from James' left confirmed Shay had closed on the enemy while they were distracted.

The dust settled from the barrages, and more targets came into view. Shay spun, slashed, and kicked through the enemy's flank, even cutting through a man's wand. James grunted and leapt toward his next closest target, slamming the knife into the man's head. He wasn't sure if the wizards *weren't* using defensive magic or if they were and the gnome-crafted knife was piercing it.

He didn't have time to ask. It'd taken them hours to drive there, but it'd taken less than a minute to kill every wizard.

Find stronger enemies, Whispy Doom insisted. *Lack of use of advanced and additional modes will lead to tactical inefficiency.*

Yeah, yeah, practice like I play. I know, Coach.

Coach is incorrect designation.

What is the correct designation, then? Whispy Doom?

Most efficient designation for now.

James smirked as he surveyed the bodies. "Too many to fit in the back. Glad I brought a head bag."

Shay laughed. "You know even when I was a professional killer, I never said shit like, 'Glad I brought a head bag.'"

He shrugged. "Just trying to be practical."

They were only an hour out from the city now. They could turn the heads in for bounty credit, then drive to an airport and return home.

James frowned, not looking forward to a flight—even a short one.

Fucking planes. I need to find some portal wizard to follow me around.

Shay stared out the window, a far-off look in her eye. "You ever try asking?"

"Huh? Asking what?"

She looked James' way. "Before you couldn't communicate with Whispy Doom, but now, from what you've told me, you can have a decent conversation."

He snorted. "A decent conversation? He—or maybe she, I don't know—just tells me to kill stronger people to adapt and get pissed so I can go into more advanced modes. How is that a decent conversation? It's like having the Devil always whispering in your ear and telling you to sin."

Shay rolled her eyes. "The point is that it's self-aware and intelligent. It might have all the answers you need. I know you said you don't care, but it wouldn't hurt."

Oh, is that what this is about?

James shrugged. "I already have."

She blinked. "What?"

"I tried asking him about a week after the Council showdown. About my planet and shit."

"And?"

James snorted. "He doesn't know a lot. Just kept yammering on about how his primary directive is to strengthen me, and his secondary directive will unlock once I've achieved 'sufficient advancement.'" He grunted. "Doesn't know shit about where I came from, at least that he'll admit, just says he adapted my DNA for 'better integration into local conditions. Complained about my 'excessive autonomy leading to tactical inefficiency.'"

"What does that mean?"

"Don't know. Maybe he's supposed to be calling the shots more than me." James frowned. "I really don't know. I get the feeling he's almost as clueless as me, just acting on instinct and programming. From what I can tell, he even accepts that his name is Whispy Doom now. Gets pissy when I call him Coach, but never complains anymore about Whispy Doom."

Shay chuckled. "Aww. How cute. You've trained it." Her smile faded, and she furrowed her brow. "Secondary directive, huh? Wonder what that means. Maybe once that becomes available he'll know more."

James shrugged. "Don't know. Don't fucking care. Worry about it once he knows what it is."

Shay rolled her eyes. "Sure. Whatever you say. You have to be the least curious man I've ever known."

"I care about the shit in front of me. That keeps life—"

"Simple," Shay finished for him. She grinned.

CHAPTER THREE

A couple of days later, Trey surveyed the gathered bounty hunters of the Brownstone Agency. Although they had a team off in Vegas, every other man stood in formation behind the building. Staff Sergeant Royce and James stood in front of the formation.

Every day it's like we turn more into soldiers or Marines than bounty hunters. Shit. Don't even know if that's a bad thing. Maybe we all should have signed our asses up for the Army before the big man had to convince us to stop being criminals.

Trey smiled to himself and waited. He knew why they were all there, even if the rest of the men didn't.

Royce whispered something to James, who nodded back and grunted.

The staff sergeant stepped forward and cleared his throat. "I've been talking more to James and Trey about how everything went down with the Council. I know I haven't said much these past few weeks other than how proud I am, but I don't think that's enough."

Everyone locked their attention on the man, the raw wound from Shorty's death still fresh. Many of them had begged James to let them come along on Council seek-and-destroy missions, but he'd wanted them to concentrate on LA and Vegas while he finished off the last vestiges of the magical cabal. Trey agreed.

Royce wore a stern look, but not a frown. "We've talked a lot since I started training you in discipline, both in combat and otherwise. I've made you read a lot of Marcus Aurelius, and if you've gotten anything out of his work, it should be that the only thing we can really control is ourselves. Not our circumstances, not others, and certainly not damned fate."

Trey snorted. *Fuck. Don't I know it, if I didn't before.*

The men all nodded, but no one said a word.

"Make no mistake, men. You're in a dangerous line of work, far more than when you were criminals. You all know that even a simple bounty can turn out to be more complicated. It was the same thing when I was in the Corps." Royce shrugged. "We'd get missions, and those were supposed to be backed up with intelligence, but sometimes shit was wrong, or shit just went south. I wasn't a desk jockey or chairborne ranger. I know what it's like to lose a brother-in-arms, even when the rest of the mission went well."

A few men swallowed. Trey took a few deep breaths.

Royce pointed at Trey, his brow furrowed. "Shorty sacrificed himself to save another man. He accomplished what a lot of men who take up arms will not be able to do. He got to choose the time and place of his death, and he got to choose a death that had some damned meaning. An honorable death."

A few murmurs of "damned right" and "fuck, yeah, Shorty" followed.

James stood, his arms crossed, watching the staff sergeant.

"We mourn the dead, and that is good. That's right to do." Royce shook his head. "But we shouldn't diminish what Shorty did or feel sorry that he made a choice to save another man. We should honor his bravery. Honor his choice. Honor that he died defending his friend, his country, and his planet from sons of bitches who thought they could do whatever they wanted.

"Shorty, along with each of you, went to the Council and their wizards and witches and monsters, and you made it clear that, 'You don't get to do what the fuck you want just because you have a little magic.' You went to these assholes who thought they could set up a base in our country, and you said, 'America doesn't bend the knee to terrorists and criminals just because they have wands.'"

"Hell, yeah!" the men chorused.

The drill instructor waited for the excited murmurs to die down. "That's what it means to be a true warrior. You don't go seeking death. If anything, it's like General Patton said: the best situation is to kill the other son of a bitch. Today, though, we honor the next best choice." He nodded to Trey.

Trey took another deep breath and stepped forward. He turned to face the men. "So, I was talking to Staff Sergeant and the big man. We ain't the military. We don't have no fancy medals and shit to hand out. Shorty don't get to be buried in Arlington." He shrugged. "But that don't mean we ain't got no way to honor him. To pay our motherfucking respects to a man who paid the ultimate price."

Another "hell, yeah" thundered from the men.

Trey pointed to the maze of walls and towers they'd been using for anti-magic training. "We've been calling that Fort Brownstone. The big man says we can officially name it 'Fort Shorty.' He even paid for this fine-ass fancy plaque that explains just who Shorty was and what he done for me and America." He shrugged. "But y'all have to agree. This ain't me delivering shit from on high. So, what do you think…we have a Fort Shorty now?"

The men cheered, hooted, and hollered.

With a smile, he turned toward Royce and James. "Looks like they think it's a good idea."

Royce nodded, and James cracked a smile.

Trey grinned. "Thought you would say that. I'll go get the plaque, and we'll get that bastard up on the wall of Fort Shorty."

As he headed toward the door, a wave of positive feelings made his entire body feel light. It wasn't as if he had expected the rest of the men to say no, but at the same time, it was hard to forget that Shorty had sacrificed himself for Trey.

I best be living a life that you won't give me shit about when I check out and join you, huh, Shorty?

Trey thought back to their discussions of the future. He'd convinced himself that just because he no longer assumed he would die young, he'd been thinking about the future, but in truth, he hadn't put thought into how to live, only how to not die.

Thoughts of Zoe bubbled up again.

Why was I saving myself? Because I didn't want some woman to have to throw herself over my coffin crying? But I gave it up to Zoe. Damned fine woman, and damned fine sex.

Trey opened the door and made his way down the hallway. The plaque was sitting in the reception area on his aunt's desk.

Did that shit with Zoe even mean anything? She said how I was great and how she got all that energy and shit, but the few times I've tried to call her these last few weeks, she said she was busy.

He snorted and shook his head. He couldn't be sure.

Women. It didn't matter if they were witches or not. They remained the world's greatest mystery.

James was barely paying attention to the podcast as he drove home in his F-350. The setting sun painted the sky orange and pink. If he hadn't been in a funk, he might have even appreciated it. Every once in a while, a word or sentence would catch his attention, and he'd pay attention for a few lines.

"A sauce revolution," declared the podcast's host. "That's what we're in the middle of. Don't let traditionalists blind you to new possibilities. All modern cuisine uses ingredients from different places. Barbeque must continue to move forward. Innovation doesn't mean ignoring what we have. It simply means improving on it."

Fuck. I'm having trouble concentrating. Why? It's not Shay.

She goes out on tomb raids all the time. It's got to be something else. This isn't me being mopey and shit.

His stomach knotted, and he grunted. James tapped his touchscreen to stop the podcast, a harsh realization taking over his mind.

A year. It'd been a year, and he hadn't even remembered. He grunted in frustration.

Over a year since those fuckers had killed Leeroy.

James gritted his teeth. One of his few disappointments was that he had so thoroughly destroyed the Harriken. While he didn't fixate on the death of his dog, the few times it did drift up in his mind, his murderous intensity returned and he wished he could go find a house filled with Harriken to rip apart. Whatever Harriken remained had long since drifted to other gangs. After all, their headquarters had been destroyed during a brutal assault by James and Shay that was capped off with magical explosives.

Maybe I should have killed all their asses sooner rather than waiting for the fuckers to keep coming at me.

Leeroy had been one of James' few true friends for years, someone who accepted him for what he was. He valued Father McCartney, but the man was his priest and confessor, not his friend. The priest had the responsibility of saving James' soul, and that brought with it a certain distance.

Although James now had more friends and family, even setting aside Father McCartney, a small hole remained in his heart. Most younger men outlived their dogs, but few had to deal with them being killed by gangsters because of something they'd done.

I wish I could have been there that night to get those bastards right then and there. I don't know if there's a dog heaven, Leeroy, but I got them. I fucking got them all. They paid for what they did to you.

James turned the corner hard, his hands tight around the wheel. He was almost to his street and his house, one that was only months old because his previous home had been destroyed by an asshole with a rocket launcher. Another thing taken from him because dumbass criminals couldn't learn their fucking lesson.

The situation was different now. Everyone told him so. Senator Johnston. Maria. Even Tyler. They all told him that people feared him now, so much so that a lot of high-level bounties avoided LA entirely rather than risk the wrath of the Granite Ghost, the Scourge of Harriken, the Council Slayer. The low-level scum thought he wouldn't stoop to beating them down, but he had the agency to do that.

Good. I want them fucking afraid. I want them all fucking afraid that I'll show up one day in their town and put them through a fucking wall.

His growing reputation brought frustration with it.

If I'd had that kind of rep back then, those Harriken fuckers wouldn't have dared touch Leeroy.

Something darted in front of the truck, and James slammed on the brakes and swerved hard.

Fuck, fuck, fuck.

No thump. Nothing but the screech of the tires until the vehicle came to a stop. His heart pounded. James didn't mind killing people who had it coming, like asshole bounties, but killing some poor bastard who happened to run in front of his truck was different.

I protect. That's what I do.

James shifted into park and threw open his door. No. It wasn't a person—at least a person who walked on two legs. It'd been quick. Dark fur, he was sure of it, and a tail.

Fuck, fuck, fuck. Please tell me I didn't hit a dog. That's not fucking funny. I don't even care if it was a shifter. That's still messed up.

James jerked his head back and forth for any sign of a wounded animal or blood. Nothing. He started circling the truck: no dents, no blood, no paint chips. It didn't look like he'd so much as scraped even a small animal.

Thank God.

He took a deep breath and slowly let it out, spotting a large form in the distance. Even in the twilight, it was clear that it was a big dog sprinting away from the area.

James rubbed the back of his neck. If it could still run like that, he obviously hadn't hit the animal.

Why the fuck was the dog just wandering the streets? Its owner should take better damn care... Wait. What if it's a stray?

James stared after the dog as it disappeared. Leeroy had been a stray, too. Even when he wasn't anymore, Leeroy liked to get out of the house every now and again. His escape and return had brought Alison into James' life.

He let out a long, weary sigh.

Was a year enough time to mourn a lost pet? A lost best friend?

Maybe it was time to get a new dog, but James wasn't sure if he was ready for the responsibility of another pet.

Fuck. It can't be that hard. I've got a teenage daughter.

After a few seconds, he grunted.

Nah. Dogs are harder than daughters, especially when your daughter is in boarding school. Then again, she's half-Drow.

James shook his head and stepped back into his truck, mental pictures of different dog breeds flipping through his mind's eye.

Shay was right. I am mopey and shit, but I know one good way to fix that problem that won't require any fucking thinking at all.

His family wasn't there to cheer him up, but it didn't matter. There was one thing that could always bring a satisfied smile to James' face, no matter the situation. He'd even relied on it when fleeing hordes of assassins brought on by a massive Harriken hit contract on his life.

It's fucking barbeque time.

CHAPTER FOUR

The swirling portal grew from a pinpoint to a vast vortex covering half the chamber.

He Who Hunts pointed a wispy tendril. "Go."

His army of misshapen monsters surged through, followed by their master and other wizards he'd summoned from distant outposts. It wasn't as if he were completely unreasonable. He hadn't twisted every wizard left in the employ of the Council, but the mutated men, now infused with his powerful essence, would be far more effective weapons than the few weak magic users he had allowed to retain their will.

The wizards followed. He hadn't told them where he found his new monsters. Perhaps they knew. He didn't care. None dared leave, and none dared challenge him.

He Who Hunts emerged into abandoned subway tunnels. Trash and debris littered the area and a dozen ragged, dirty humans cowered against the wall, shaking, their eyes wide, too panicked to even flee. It was too late now. Wizards and monsters blocked their escape routes on either side.

"Who?" he rasped, "are you?"

One of the men stumbled forward, trembling like an earthquake was occurring. "We're nothing. We just stay here because we ain't got nowhere else to go."

He Who Hunts floated closer. The man's teeth started chattering.

"Homeless, yes? No one to miss you, then."

The man's lip quivered. "We just wanted to sleep where there ain't no wind. Please, sir. I ain't ever said a bad word about Oricerans. That's what you are, right? An Oriceran?"

He Who Hunts stopped advancing. "You could be useful. Human society has discarded you, ignored you. I could turn you into something greater."

The man stopped shaking and took a few deep breaths. "Something more? Y-you gonna give me some Oriceran magic?"

He Who Hunts felt no compulsion to clarify his true origins. It amused him that the man thought he was a mere Oriceran.

The homeless man glanced over his shoulder at the other homeless gathered. Several looked excited now, but most still wore terrified masks.

"Magic," He Who Hunts echoed, his voice as raspy as ever. "Life is magic. Do you know that?" He let out a hollow laugh.

The homeless man gave a nervous chuckle and shrugged. "I don't know much about no magic. I-I want to learn. I always told everyone, from the beginning, when you all came over from Oriceran that it was a good thing.

That Earth would be a better place. I've always been pro-Oriceran. You can ask anyone. Honest to God. I like magic."

"Good." He Who Hunts shoved a tendril into the man's heart.

His flesh sizzled and burned as his scream echoed.

"Please," the man screamed, falling to his knees. "Please show mercy."

A light red glow surrounded the man, the energy flowing in pulses through the tendril embedded in the man's chest.

He Who Hunts floated down until his eyes stared directly into the human's. "You don't understand. This *is* my mercy. I give you purpose in your death. I'm making you useful. I don't ignore you or make you sleep in tunnels. You are part now of a glorious plan."

The other homeless turned to flee, only to be boxed in by the wizards and monsters. Some howled their outrage. Others began sobbing.

He Who Hunts continued to feed. A snack, really. The man didn't have a speck of magical ability, but at least his lifeforce could provide some small sustenance.

His victim's eyes glazed over and he slumped forward, his breathing stopping. His skin began to shrivel and split.

The murderous cloud of red mist rose into the air from He Who Hunts' body, his tendril still impaling the homeless man. "You aren't dying today. You're becoming part of something greater."

He tossed the man to the ground and shot toward another screaming victim.

He Who Hunts turned toward his servants. "I will feed,

and you will prepare. Soon, we will give Brownstone his first test."

They nodded, none changing their expressions as the screams and sobs echoed around them.

Maria glanced down at the black evening gown, liking what it did for her body. Decades of conditioning had given her a firm, toned body rather than a voluptuous silhouette, but Tyler didn't seem to mind, and he was the main person seeing her naked these days.

She picked up her wine glass and took a sip, shooting a smile at Tyler across the table. The man filled out a suit well. Even when he was at the Black Sun, he tended toward nice silk shirts and vests, always going for the upscale bartender look.

He's handsomer than he thinks, but I don't want to feed his ego by telling him that.

"How's the wine?" Tyler asked.

Maria set it down. "Good. Don't know if it's worth as much as they're charging you, but it beats the crap I get from the grocery store."

Tyler chuckled. "Well, I thought a nice dinner might be in order. As fun as take-out and a movie at your place is, it's nice to dress up." His gaze roamed her body. "For both of us."

Damn, boy. Save it until we're out of the restaurant.

She hoped her cheeks didn't look as red as they felt. "Is that the only reason?"

Tyler shook his head. "No. You have seemed a little...off lately. I thought it might get your mind off things."

Maria chuckled. "Off?"

"Yeah. Ever since the Council base raid wrapped up. It's like you're not all there." Tyler made a circular gesture with his hand. "I'm an information broker. It's my job to notice things about people, and I'd be a shitty boyfriend if I didn't notice something's bothering you."

She laughed. "It's still weird to hear that."

Tyler furrowed his brow. "What?"

"That you're my boyfriend." Maria shrugged. "I've mostly dated cops, but it's gotten harder the higher up I've gone, and it's hard to find a man even in the force who isn't intimidated by a ball-busting AET lieutenant." She let out a long sigh. "Sometimes I just wonder."

"About what?" Tyler downed the rest of his glass of wine and refilled it from the bottle sitting in ice in the middle of the table.

Maria shrugged. "The force. I've been a cop since I got out of college. It's weird to think I'm in my forties, and I've been doing this for so long. This leave of absence has given me time to think."

Tyler frowned and looked over his shoulder. "I'm thinking about the fact that I'm paying a shitload of money for this meal, and they're taking forever to deliver the entrees. Those appetizers weren't very filling. That's the problem with fancy food. Ten times the price for one-tenth the size."

Maria gave him a death stare.

He held up a hand. "I'm still listening. Just hungry. Didn't eat all day. Figured if I was hungrier it'd make the expensive food tastier, but what about your leave of absence?" He picked up his glass.

"I'm thinking about resigning."

Tyler slowly set his glass down, watching Maria with obvious disbelief in his eyes. "What?"

Yeah, didn't see that coming, did you, Mr. Information-Broker Boyfriend?

Maria shrugged. "I love being a cop. I love protecting people, and I love taking down overpowered assholes who are threatening innocent people, but the politicians, and all the higher-up brass who are sucking up to the politicians—they make everything impossible. I'm losing men, and the asshole politicians are more worried about budgets than dead cops—or hell, dead civilians." She shook her head. "I'm not going to lie. Working that mission with Brownstone felt good. *Damned* good."

Tyler frowned. "I don't know if I like where this is going."

Maria leaned forward. "We were kicking ass and taking out the bad guys, just like I do with AET, but there wasn't all the political crap. We just armed up with what we needed, tracked down the assholes, and took them out. It felt very freeing."

"Well, fine, quit then." Tyler shrugged. "You're kickass. It's not like you needed Brownstone to know that. There are different ways to help people." He took another sip of wine. "You could be a security consultant. Sit back, tell people what they want to hear, and make money. Hell, tell them what they need to hear but don't want to believe because they've been too cheap before. It'll be so easy, it should be illegal."

Maria shook her head. "No, not yet. I can't."

"Can't quit?"

"No, can't take that kind of desk job." She frowned. "I've got another ten years of fieldwork in me yet. I want to be hands-on, not just some consultant running around telling museum assholes to fix obvious holes in their security."

Tyler rubbed his chin. "Why not start your own security firm then? You can hire people and lead from the front."

"I'm not a businesswoman. I've been a cop half my life. It's all I know how to do. Even my degree is in criminology. There's no way I can build a successful business from the ground up, even with contacts."

Damn, I sound pathetic. At least he's not giving me the pity look. That'd be too much.

Tyler picked up his glass to take a sip. "Look, I might have a...different sort of business, but I do understand business, and any business is all about opportunities. I'm sure you can get contracts set up with the feds or something, if only because of all that shit you did with the Council, Brownstone, and Shay. It'll be easier than you think."

Brownstone...

Maria's heart rate kicked up, and her eyes widened. "That's it."

He smiled. "Yeah. See? It's just about thinking about it differently. New perspective and all that."

She shook her head so hard she got a few looks from nearby tables. "No, Brownstone's the key. Don't you get it?"

Tyler frowned. "No, I *don't* get it. What? You want to use Brownstone's connections?"

Maria snorted. "No. Screw starting my own business. I told you earlier that working with him made me feel free. He's already *got* a business, and he already goes after the worst scum. I'd be saving myself time and not just babysitting some corporate business jerk who pissed off too many protestors. I'd be helping take down real threats."

"You've got be kidding me." Tyler set down his glass and scrubbed his face with his hand. "You can't possibly be thinking of working with Brownstone. You used to hate the guy."

Maria rolled her eyes. "In case you didn't notice, shit changed. Why do you care so much? I thought stuff changed for you, too. I thought you were friends."

Tyler held up a finger. "More like frenemies, but that's not the point."

"What *is* the point, then?"

Tyler sighed. "That guy's trouble. It's like God decided to test out new Horsemen of the Apocalypse on Brownstone first or some crap like that. You join up with him, you'll be in danger all that time. And…" He sighed. "I don't like that hungry gleam in your eye."

Maria's expression softened. "If anything, working with Brownstone will be safer than working as the tactical head of the AET."

"How the hell do you figure?"

She smirked and gulped down half her glass. "Because I was always dealing with funding and equipment requisition issues. At least if I'm working with Brownstone, I'll always have him backing me up in the end. Money can't buy that level of backup."

"Still don't like it," Tyler grumbled. "Just think about it."

"Sure, I'll think about it." Maria nodded past him. "Looks like our food's here."

Tyler grunted. "Finally. What? Did they actually take a boat out into the ocean to catch the fish on order?"

Trey adjusted his tie as he stood in front of Zoe's door.

Damn. Should I be doing this? I mean, she took my energy and shit. Don't that make her like a succubus or something? But damn, was that good sex, and that rack...fuck. That's got to be magical.

He shook his head. "Fuck it. If I can take on dangerous bounties, I can hit on a woman I've already slept with." He knocked on the door.

A moment later, the door swung open, and Zoe stood there in a white silk robe, her eyes bloodshot. A thin smile appeared on her face. "Hello, Trey," she slurred.

Fruity wine notes accompanied her breath. Trey still didn't understand why she needed to get so blitzed to do most of her magic, but there was a lot about the arcane arts he didn't understand.

He rubbed the back of his neck. "Maybe this ain't the best time to chat."

Zoe laughed. "Why? Because I'm drunk?" She winked. "Oh, I'm drunk most of the time, my little supernova. You'll have to get used to that."

Trey chuckled. "Supernova? I like the sound of that."

She pulled the door farther open with a merry smile and nodded inside. "Please join me."

He stepped inside, careful to avoid any of the pots on

the ground or the hanging pots above. As with every other time he'd been there, the plants covered the range from the normal and green to the moving and glowing.

Zoe closed the door behind her and leaned back against it, part of her robe slipping off and revealing one of her shoulders. She licked her lips. "I'm glad you came back."

Trey tried to avoid a frown, but he couldn't resist crossing his arms. "Oh?"

Is she just playing me now?

"Yes. I've been busy with orders, but I've found myself thinking back again and again to my time with you." She shuddered, her eyes half-closed. "I wish I could explain how fantastic it was."

Trey grinned and shrugged. "You know, maybe I'm just like the Mozart of fucking."

Zoe giggled, lifting her hand to her face. "Perhaps. I will admit that part was satisfying, but you are a man of unusually potent energy." She took in and let out a few deep breaths. "And a witch could get addicted to both aspects of that." She leaned forward. "Even though I should know better than to toy with anyone in the orbit of James Brownstone."

Trey frowned. He wanted to be with Zoe, but he wouldn't spend time with any woman who disrespected James. The man had done so much for Trey, and as with Shorty, he would never let himself forget.

"What do you have against the big man? I mean, you sell him potions and shit."

She waved a hand. "No, no, no. You misunderstand. James isn't a man I'd count as an enemy. He's just very dangerous, and by extension everyone around him is dangerous." She took a shuddering breath and swallowed. "I won't lie. I do want you, Trey. I tell myself you live a dangerous life, and he'll drag you into a *more* dangerous life, but I also know that you aren't the raging inferno he is. I could experience glories both magical and sexual with you...and not be destroyed."

Trey chuckled. "That's the weirdest fucking come-on line I've ever heard." He shrugged. "But I'm not gonna sit here and lie. You're damn fine, and shit, I can't get you out of my fucking head, but I also am kind of sensing here that you're not used to settling down with one man."

Zoe barked a laugh. "A proper Dionysian revel is a glorious carnival of the basest pleasures. No, I'm not one who usually confines myself to a single man, or woman for that matter."

"Damn." Trey shrugged. "That's a fuckload of competition. I ain't saying I can play like that, Zoe. This shit is serious to me." He scrunched his forehead. "Well, shit's serious to you, too, but it's special to me, you know what I'm saying? If I'm gonna be with you, I need to know you're not fucking everyone in sight. If that's too much for you, no harm, no foul. We all got to do what we got to do. I'm just telling you what I can handle."

She sighed. "I will admit most of my magical energy comes more from the drinking than sex. It'd be a...difficult adjustment. I've also lived this way for a long time."

Trey stared at her. "How long we talking? You don't look so old."

Zoe gave him a coy smile. "I was friends with Mata Hari. Now *there* was a woman who knew how to party."

"Damn." Trey blinked several times after doing a few

quick calculations in his head. At the minimum, she was over a hundred years old, but she looked like she was in her mid-twenties.

Talk about a GILF, but damn, she's hotter than fuck. She's cradle-robbing with me. Still, she talks about getting addicted to me, and I think I'm already addicted to her, but I need to play this shit cool. She's hot, way older than me, and magical. Talk about having all the power in the relationship.

Trey cleared his throat, looking her up and down, his gaze lingering on an exposed thigh. She sure knew how to work a white silk robe.

"You would look *damn* good even if you were like a quarter of how old I think you are."

Zoe sashayed forward and wrapped her arms around his neck, licking her lips. "You're special, I think. Worth the sacrifice."

He grinned. "Not gonna argue with the expert."

"A challenge, then." Her breath hitched, and Trey found himself transfixed by the rise and fall of her exposed cleavage. "Satisfy me enough to prove I need no one else. Break me, and then I'll consider being exclusive to you. I'll even make this easy. I'll deny myself others in the meantime to give you a chance to prove that it's worth it."

Trey leaned forward, his lips almost brushing hers. "Challenge accepted."

CHAPTER FIVE

James stepped out of Phillips Bar-B-Que, still gnawing on a rib, a plastic bag filled with more protein goodness for later at home and tomorrow. His mind and heart were at ease, the beast soothed by massive amounts of sauced meat.

Don't know why Shay doesn't get that this is the best shit people ever created. Better than fucking penicillin, even.

He grunted. Maybe not that, but at least a close second.

His hair stood up on the back of his head, and a loud buzz sounded from behind him. James turned around.

A swirling portal appeared, tinged red at the edges. Four men in slacks and dark shirts stepped through, all holding wands at their sides. The portal winked shut behind them.

Wizards? I hope they're just hungry.

James took a final bite of his rib and let it fall into his bag. "Who the fuck are you?"

The wizards all whipped their wands up and chanted in unison in a language he didn't understand.

Lacking bonding to Whispy Doom, James wasn't cocky enough to think he could take a direct hit from four wizards. He leapt to the side as four firebolts screamed past him and smashed into the wall, exploding, and showering the parking lot with drywall, wood, and bits of metal. He kept running until he could duck behind a huge dumpster at the back of the parking lot.

Several people screamed inside and ran toward the back, but no one looked hurt yet.

The owner stared at the wall from behind the counter, his eyes wide.

Those fuckers. Why did they have to get an innocent barbeque restaurant involved in this?

"If you're gonna fucking try to kill me," James shouted, "you should at least tell me who you are." He jumped again as a fireball appeared and flew toward him.

His bag of ribs slipped out of his hand to be charred beyond deliciousness by a direct hit from a fireball.

James growled. These assholes were really starting to get on his nerves. He whipped out his .45. It didn't matter if they had bounties or not, now that he was solidly in self-defense territory.

He spun around the corner and opened fire. A wizard's head exploded and another jerked back, blood spraying his neck. James' bullets intended for the third and fourth man melted into vapor several inches away from the targets. James kept firing, but the wizards' shields kept them alive.

The bounty hunter returned to cover in time to avoid another firebolt, but a second aerial fireball landed right next to him and exploded. He hissed at the ache on his burned side. The smell of charred cotton and flesh filled his nostrils.

The amulet rested comfortably against his chest but remained separated by the metal spacer. If he pulled it off he could begin bonding with it, but he'd be vulnerable for several seconds, and he wasn't sure if he could take a direct hit during the process.

As if the wizards could read his thoughts, they sent two fireballs at him. He rolled back, the motion rubbing his wounded side against the ground, and growled.

No. There wouldn't be enough time to bond with Whispy Doom while the assholes were on him. He had rounds left in his magazine, but he would have to go for the backup gear he kept in his truck.

Can't risk those fuckers hurting the F-350. I don't know how long my mechanic can keep fixing it if I get it blown up again.

James waited a few seconds for more fireballs to appear and sprinted around the corner. This time he took two measured, slow shots at the wizards. The bullets didn't pierce their defenses any better than the quick shots. Keeping himself moving, he fired a couple more times.

The wizards' faces twitched with each shot.

They probably can't shoot back when I'm firing at them, which means they might be vulnerable when they take a shot.

By his count, seven shots remained in his magazine. He eyed his truck for a brief second, his heart pounding. The fuckers had already burned his ribs, damaged one of his favorite barbeque restaurants, and now even his beloved truck might be harmed.

Assholes. I will fucking end you. I was fucking trying to relax!

Loud sirens sang in the distance, obviously closing.

He didn't care about waiting for the cops. The wizard assholes had tried to kill him, and now they were going to pay for it.

James rushed down the parking lot, looking over his shoulder and waiting. One of the wizards launched a fire-bolt, and he returned fire almost instantly. His enemy fell with a scream, but the fire magic slammed into James' shoulder, sending him spiraling to the ground with a grunt and charred flesh.

He shoved himself to the side as he hit the ground. His instincts served him well when a fireball slammed right into where he'd been just a second before.

With a loud growl, he hopped to his feet and opened up with his gun, letting loose three quick shots. The bullets melted, as before, but didn't vaporize. Instead, they became glowing super-hot lead, a shotgun blast of molten metal to the face, neck, and chest of the wizard.

The wizard howled in pain and fell to the ground. His wand dropped out of his hand and rolled away.

James growled and stomped forward, the agony in his shoulder and side building. He kept moving forward until he was a couple of yards away, raised his gun, and emptied the last few rounds into the screaming wizard until the man stopped moving.

He holstered his weapon and pulled a healing potion out of what remained of his jacket, then fell to his knees and downed the potion. His poor clothes remained charred and full of holes, but his burns healed quickly and the pain vanished.

James looked at the bodies. He didn't recognize any of them, and he never forgot a face. They weren't in any sort of uniform.

Three huge drones with flashing red and white lights zoomed into the area.

"This is the LAPD," announced a voice over a loudspeaker in one of the drones. "Put your hands on your head."

James shook his head and complied. He didn't have time to piss the cops off.

Ten minutes later, AET Sergeant Weber stood in front of James in full armor with his helmet off. "And you have no idea who might have wanted to kill you?"

The minute the AET showed up and realized it was Brownstone they stood down, but now the entire area was filled with cops, CSIs, and firefighters inspecting the damage to the restaurant.

James shrugged. "Nope. They didn't say shit, and I killed them all before I could ask any questions. They were wizards."

Sergeant Weber groaned. "That doesn't really narrow it down. Can you give us a list of possible suspects?"

"Sure, but it'd be a pretty damned long list. I've taken down a lot of wizards over the last few years."

The cop nodded and nodded to the bodies. "No one else got hurt except them. It's a miracle."

James pointed to the restaurant. "They fucked that place up."

"Yeah, but at least all the customers and the employees are all right." Sergeant Weber shook his head. "You sure there's not some new contract on you? Like with the Harriken?"

James shrugged. "Don't know. Not that I've heard. Fuck, you know how I work. If I knew assholes were after me, I wouldn't be going where anyone other than assholes could be hurt."

The cop nodded. "Let us know if anything comes up, not that you can't handle this kind of thing yourself. Anyway, I've got to go check on some things."

James gave him a nod, and Sergeant Weber wandered off.

The owner of Phillips Bar-B-Que sat on the curb in front of his restaurant, his head in his hands.

James marched over to him. "You okay?"

The man looked up. "I already called my insurance company. They said because it's magical damage, they don't have to pay. I don't have the right kind of insurance. They're not even going to send an adjuster out."

"Fuckers." James shook his head. "Don't worry, I'll pay for all the repairs. Shit, if you want to throw in a remodel, I'll pay for that, too."

The owner blinked several times. "What? You serious?"

"Damn right, I'm serious. These fuckers were after me, and there's no way I'm gonna let a barbeque place go under because it got caught in the crossfire. It's the least I can do."

"I..." The owner took a deep breath. "I'm not going to say no, but it's going to be pretty expensive."

James shrugged. "Big fucking deal. Just give me the estimate, and I'll get the money."

He resisted the urge to point out he probably spent more on one anti-magic deflector than the entire building cost—although at least with the deflectors, as long as they weren't destroyed they could regain their power.

A weary smile appeared on the owner's face. "Remodel too, huh? Don't like the old décor?"

James grunted. "Just saying, you haven't changed it in a long time."

He looked at the bodies. Police camera drones were floating around taking pictures at different angles. He was glad the wizards were dead.

Few things in life are unforgivable: fucking with his family, fucking with his friends, and fucking with his barbeque.

Hours later, James sighed as he leaned back on his couch. He wondered if he should tell Shay that someone was trying to kill him—again. If he did, she'd freak out and rush back from her tomb raid. He didn't need a babysitter, but he wasn't sure if the situation fell under what his relationship podcasts described as "maintaining open and honest channels of communication."

No reason to call her right away. The wizards are dead, and no one has shown up at my house. They might have been it.

Find enemies. Kill them. Grow stronger.

James grunted. He'd bonded with Whispy just to be prepared, but he didn't know how long he could actually take the damn thing whispering in his mind and making demands. It wasn't like he could wear it twenty-four/seven. Sometimes the amulet would keep quiet on the way to a mission, but obviously, he didn't like sitting around doing nothing.

Shut the fuck up. If you want me to find the enemy, there are some people I need to talk to first.

The amulet didn't respond.

The police had already called him to tell him they had no good leads. The victims' DNA couldn't be matched to any public database, nor could their fingerprints or faces. It was hard for people to be totally hidden from the system, but when magic was involved it wasn't as surprising.

If the police couldn't help him, he would have to use his own resources. If the men weren't in databases, that would limit Heather's ability to help him—or Peyton's for that matter, but he also would prefer to ask from help from someone who wouldn't immediately leak it to Shay. He *did* plan to tell her, just when the time was right.

Okay, I'll get Heather going and bring in some reinforcements.

James did know one man with connections to the underworld, both mundane and magical, who might be able to find out who was after him as long as he was paid.

Taking a deep breath, James picked up the phone and dialed Tyler.

The information broker answered after the second ring. "Is whatever you're about to ask going to make me money?"

James grunted. "This shit is straightforward. Just need information, and I'll pay for it. Someone tried to kill me a few hours ago. I killed them before I could find out why or who."

Tyler laughed. "Yeah, I heard about that, but I figured if you ever go out, it's not going to be in the parking lot of some barbeque place." He paused for a few beats. "Huh. Then again, maybe that would make perfect sense."

"Whatever. Just fucking find out who."

"This is going to cost you." Tyler chuckled. "And if you want it fast, I'm going to have to tack on some sort of premium service fee."

"Just fucking find out. The sooner, the better."

James frowned. Maybe the whole thing was a waste of time. The four wizards might have been the only ones left in whatever conspiracy to assassinate him.

Tyler let out a breath. "Hey, while I've got you on the phone, I've got a few questions."

"Is this shit gonna take long?"

"What? You got something better to do? You just admitted you don't even know who to go after, so it sounds like you need me more than I need you." Tyler chuckled.

James grunted. "Just fucking ask already."

"You ever thought about building up your agency more? I mean you've got Trey and his guys, but you've also got a nice reputation now. You guys won against the Council when other top bounty hunters couldn't pull it off so it might be a good time to expand beyond just ex-gang-bangers."

James frowned. "Trey and his boys are good bounty hunters. It doesn't mean shit that they used to be in a gang."

"Not saying that. Just saying you could pick up some

quality people right now, and you should think about the future. Trust me. I know a thing or two about expanding a business."

James furrowed his brow, suspicion flowing through him. Why did Tyler care so much about Brownstone Agency's staffing?

He was about to ask when something very different came out, "Shit. We don't always have enough men to handle every job. The higher-end bounties are avoiding LA, but it's almost like there are more lower-end bounties now."

"Yep," Tyler replied. "Plus, you need to build up your anti-magic experience and capabilities. You can't be everywhere at once." A faint tremor in his voice reignited James' suspicions. "You should pay a good premium for that sort of thing; someone with that kind of experience."

James sighed. "I'll think about it, but I can't worry about that shit right now. I need to figure out who is trying to kill me first."

"Yeah, yeah. I'll find out. After all, I'm curious anyway."

"Curious about what?"

"Who is such a dumb shit that they're willing to go after you in LA? Talk to you soon."

Tyler ended the call.

James held out his phone and stared at it for a second, again wondering why Tyler was so insistent on discussing staffing. Given the man's history, this had to be part of some sort of money-making scheme.

Fuck him if he thinks I'm going to hire anyone to do pay-per-view bounties.

James lay down and closed his eyes, but a few minutes later he sat up and shook his head.

I can't keep putting this shit off. It'll just make it worse.

He reached over and picked up his phone, hesitating for a moment before dialing Shay.

Maybe I'll get lucky, and she'll be in some cave where she won't even be able to get reception.

"I was waiting for you to call," she answered.

"Not in a cave, huh?"

Shay laughed. "Nope. At a hotel. We're hitting the site tomorrow morning."

Not so lucky after all.

James rubbed the back of his head. "And why were you waiting for me to call?"

"I have alerts set up for unusual crimes in Los Angeles County. Sometimes I even have Peyton keep an eye on that sort of thing, but he's on vacation with his girlfriend, so I just used my meager efforts—not that it was hard." Shay snickered. "But unless the report I saw was very much mistaken, you blew up a barbeque restaurant in a firefight."

"I would never blow up a barbeque restaurant," James snarled. "The fuckers who tried to kill me did."

"Okay, calm down there. Don't go all crazy on me for insulting the honor of barbeque." She sighed. "Seriously, though, who the fuck is trying to kill you now?"

"I'll tell you what I told the cops. Don't know. I've got Tyler looking into it. You don't need to come back."

"And Alison?"

James groaned. "She doesn't need to worry."

Shay snorted. "She deserves to know. She's not a little kid anymore. The minute you started taking her on bounties, you went way past 'have to protect her from the truth' land."

"Fine. I'll fucking call her. Just not tonight. I'm still pissed about the whole thing."

"Because someone tried to kill you?"

James grunted. "Nah. Lots of people try to kill me. Why couldn't they have tried to fucking kill me in front of a frozen yogurt place instead of a barbeque place?"

Shay laughed so hard James had to pull the phone away from his ear for a few seconds.

The cackling turned into mere chuckling. "I don't think I've ever seen you eat frozen yogurt."

"Just saying." James glanced at his nightstand. The amulet lay there, the separator off, just in case he needed a quick bonding in the middle of the night. "I'm gonna get going."

"Okay. Be careful. Don't be a dumbass, and don't get yourself killed. I'm heading straight home with Lily after this tomb raid. It seems like I can't take my eyes off you for a minute without something trying to murder you."

James chuckled. "I'm a real love-or-hate kind of guy."

CHAPTER SIX

S hay picked up a rock and threw it against the rocky face of Mount Hallasan right in front of her. The stone disappeared, and a wide area of the wall rippled like the surface of the water.

"Looks like we're here."

At least something's gone right.

Shay muttered and cursed under her breath as she stepped through the wall into a dark cave, which was a vast lava tube. Her headlamp pierced the darkness to reveal stalactites and stalagmites running down the tube mouth, which gave the whole area a resemblance to the maw of a giant monster.

Yeah, not creepy at all.

The scabbard of her *tachi* clacked against the rock formations as she moved through them.

"You're mumbling again," Lily called from behind her, a slight smirk on her face. The false wall rippled as she stepped past.

Shay looked over her shoulder and shrugged. "Just pissed that I go away and he immediately gets in trouble."

Lily shrugged. "It's not like he can't take care of himself. The guy's like a one-man army."

Shay shook her head. "He always says that, but I've had to save his ass plenty of times. No one's an island and all that shit."

The teen Gray Elf laughed, her eyes lit up in amusement.

Shay frowned. "What's so fucking funny?"

"Just you. You've...changed." Lily shrugged.

Shay looked at Lily. She wasn't the only one who had changed. Her protégé was far more toned and fit than when Shay had first met her. She even walked with more confidence. Combined with her existing magical abilities, Lily was turning into the perfect tomb raider.

"Everyone changes. Hopefully, they just change for the better." Shay shrugged. "I'll stop bitching about him now, so we can concentrate on the tomb raid." She stepped farther into the cool and moist cave. "Get any visions?"

Lily shook her head. "Nothing. Other than that guy getting sick at breakfast, haven't seen much."

Shay chuckled and nodded. "You helped save my jacket from a fate worse than death. I appreciate it."

The entire job was already strange. They'd been hired to go to Jeju Island off the coast of South Korea to recover a magical glass jug, specifically a glass ewer associated with the bath rituals of the founder of one the ancient Korean precursor kingdoms, Silla. The ewer had been kept by Silla Royalty, but lost with the fall of the kingdom. Allegedly, it possessed magical healing powers and no one had a record of it, even in rumor, for over a millennium. Just recently, a Korean shaman had somehow discovered its location on Jeju Island, far from where it'd last been seen.

None of that was unusual for Shay, but the client was: the government of South Korea. Even though she'd been hired indirectly under her alias of Aletheia, this whole job was approaching something rather official.

It's like I'm Hollingsworth now.

She wasn't sure why it was bothering her. It wasn't like she normally chose to work for criminal scum, but the idea of working on a tomb raid for a government shortly after working on a bounty for another government agency didn't sit well.

I've come a long way from being a professional killer. I'm all mainstream and aboveboard and shit.

The Korean government had passed along the cryptic information that the shaman who had located the artifact had noted extreme magic at the site and suggested a professional tomb raider recover the item.

Wonder if that means they actually expect me to succeed, or if they just want to judge the level of danger. Doesn't matter. They're paying enough.

Shay grinned over her shoulder. "Is this making you homesick? Miss the tunnels?"

Lily rolled her eyes. "No, we like the apartments much better."

Shay's grin faded, and she nodded. "Good. You're making far too much money to be living underground. Is everything still going okay with Harry and the rest running their little information-collection business?"

"Yeah. Fine." The teen let out a quiet laugh. "It just

seems like we needed to be able to catch our breath, and once we did, everything worked itself out."

Their footsteps and voices echoed down the tube.

Shay took a moment to look around for any obvious traps before continuing deeper into the mountain. "And have you thought about what I asked you?"

Lily nodded. "About the School of Necessary Magic?"

"Yeah."

Lily sighed. "I've talked with everyone about it, and they all feel the same way I do."

"You know Alison's benefited a lot from being there." Shay shrugged. "Just something to consider."

"Even with everything strange in her life, she still grew up in a normal home situation with two parents, at least until all that crap happened." Lily shook her head. "I understand, and they all understand, that maybe we'd have more magic if we went to the school, but it just doesn't feel like the place for us."

Shay shrugged. "You're doing well for yourself already, so I can't say you're wrong. In fact, you're getting to the point where real solo raids aren't out of the question."

Lily glanced at Shay, her gray eyes widening. "You think so?"

"Yeah, between your premonitions and your reflexes, you're already more prepared for a typical tomb raid than most tomb raiders." Shay stepped around a shallow pool of fetid water. "I can talk to Peyton about setting up your own identity, and you can start building your rep. I guess I'm pulling a James. I'll just take a cut of what you're doing, but a lot of it would be you working on your own jobs."

Lily nodded, a thoughtful look on her face. "I'm probably not ready to wander around foreign countries by myself."

"Then stick closer to home as you build up experience. Just saying, it won't be that long before you're better than me." Shay smiled.

"Shay, duck!" Lily yelled.

Heart pounding, the tomb raider reacted without thought, which saved her life as a spinning blade shot from the side of the cave and passed right over her dropping head.

Shay lingered on the ground for a moment. "That was a good premonition." She reached into her backpack to fish out her AR goggles and took a moment to set them up and look at the wall. She tapped a few times on the side of the glasses.

"Whatever was messing with the drone I tried to fly around earlier isn't affecting this." The trap apparatus glowed a few degrees hotter than the surroundings. "I can make out the trap using thermal mode. Guess we're going to have to go a lot slower than..." She twisted to look down the cave. A huge humanoid signature rushed toward them. The thermal signature was blinding. "We've got company."

The thudding, echoing footsteps would have warned her even without her glasses.

Shay hopped to her feet and pulled out her gun. Lily pulled out hers as well.

A deafening roar echoed around them. Shay backed up and knelt behind a wide stalagmite, then tapped her goggles to revert to normal light mode, blinking a few times as her eyes adjusted.

A few seconds later, flickering light illuminated the

cave as a gray-skinned giant stomped around a bend in the tube. Bathed in an aura of flame, the creature had to duck to avoid some of the longer stalactites. His thick, cracked hide resembled the rock of the cave, two glowing solid-yellow eyes peered from his face, and long, sharp claws tipped his hands.

"Shit," Shay muttered. "I'd read about *dokkaebi* legends in this area, but nothing recent."

The monster bellowed again.

Damn it. I was hoping to get one of the mischievous ones, not one of the large and angry ones. Shit luck today.

"I've got no reason to fight with you," Shay shouted back, her ears still ringing.

The *dokkaebi* let out a low, deep chuckle and rattled something off in a foreign language. Shay presumed it was some Korean dialect.

Of course. Not every human speaks English, why should every monster I run into?

Shay sighed. "You don't happen to speak Korean, do you, Lily?"

The girl shook her head, her gray hair whipping around.

Shay yanked out her phone, quickly brought up her translation app, and tried again.

This time when the monster replied, the phone spat out a halting translation after a quick warning about archaic speech patterns.

The message was simple. "Trespassers must die."

Shay rose, keeping her weapon pointed and her phone in her other hand. "We've been assigned to retrieve the glass ewer of King Bak Hyeokgeose. This is an official request from the Ministry of Culture, Sports, and Tourism of the Republic of Korea. This is a legal recovery of a cultural artifact."

The monster laughed and rattled off his response, his words continuing to be translated by Shay's phone. "Humans always think words on a page mean something. Magic has returned. The world has become what it once was." He sniffed at the air. "I leave the humans below alone, and they have wisely left this cave alone. But you fools came."

Don't think they even know about it anymore, pal, but whatever.

"Like I said, we're just here for the ewer. It's a Korean cultural treasure, and they want it back."

The monster slammed a fist against his chest. "It's been so long since I've tasted human flesh. Centuries."

"Centuries, huh?" Shay grinned. "A lot of things have changed. Humans aren't as weak as they once were. Maybe *you* should be the one walking away."

The monster let out a terrifying laugh. "Enough games. Now you die."

He rushed forward, and Shay fired three quick shots at his chest. He jerked back, bright red blood streaming from his chest, and fell to his knees.

She pocketed her phone and smirked. "Now that wasn't so har—"

The *dokkaebi* stood and roared, its flames intensifying. The wound started burning, and a second later it was healed.

Shay holstered her pistol and dropped her hand to the hilt of her sword. "Can you distract the flaming Hungry, Hungry Hippo there?"

Lily nodded and took a deep breath. "Sure. This whole place is like one giant parkour course."

"Don't die. I'd hate to have you die after I gave you that big speech about you being ready to fly solo." Shay winked.

The monster charged her again, moving around some of the obstacles in his way and crashing through others, the flying rock shards pelting the cave walls.

Lily leapt on top of a stalagmite and then jumped up, spinning around a moist low-hanging stalactite, gloves protecting her hands. She let go and flew past the *dokkaebi*.

The huge monster swung at her, narrowly missing as the girl twisted her body, her preternatural reflexes saving her. She grabbed another stalactite and yanked herself up, then pushed off with her legs.

Shay took the opportunity to charge the distracted monster. She unsheathed her blade and wove around the stalagmites as she closed the distance.

The *dokkaebi* spun around, roared, and swung a claw at Shay. She dodged to the side and slashed with her sword. The blade severed the monster's forearm, splattering blood. A screaming roar followed as the huge monster flailed.

Shay ducked his remaining arm, only for him to whip it back and slam it into her. She flew back and crashed against the hard rock of the cave wall, a distinct crack preceding an explosion of utter agony in her leg.

She gritted her teeth and looked down. Her right leg

was bent at an angle that would be impressive even for Gumby, and the entire limb throbbed.

"Fuck." Shay shook her head and groped for her sword, then grabbed it. "Lily, catch!"

Her breathing ragged, the tomb raider threw the blade toward the girl. Lily rolled under the *dokkaebi's* arm and snatched the hilt while the sword was still in flight, spun, and planted the blade into the neck of the monster. He lashed out and sent her into the same wall as her mentor.

The *dokkaebi* rounded on the pair, blood spurting from his neck. He gurgled and took several ponderous steps forward before falling and impaling himself on a stalagmite. A few seconds later, the fiery aura around him died, and he slumped farther forward.

Oh, fuck, was that close. Yeah, maybe I should keep that in mind next time I lecture James.

Shay reached into a pouch on her tactical belt to pull out a healing potion. "Lily, you okay?"

The girl hissed and reached into her own belt to grab a potion as she pushed off the wall with her other arm. She fell forward, her back covered in blood. "I've been better."

Both women downed their healing potions and waited for their agony to end.

A half-minute later they both stood, the pain and injury gone.

Shay sighed and walked over to grab her *tachi.* "That could have gone better. I don't just need a healing potion. I need a pain potion half the time. *Damn*, does that shit hurt."

Lily shrugged and patted her back. Her jacket had a massive hole where jagged rocks had pierced it. "We're not dead. That's a win, right?

Shay slid down her AR goggles. "Let's just hope the next trap and monsters show up as obviously on IR." She shook her head. "I just want to get this shit over so I can get back to LA and save James' ass."

CHAPTER SEVEN

A half-hour more of wandering brought Shay and Lily in contact with ten more traps, but no more giant monsters. Between the AR goggles and Lily's occasional premonitions, they escaped any further injury, which was fine by Shay since she and Lily each only had a single potion left.

After they turned a corner, Shay was nearly blinded by an intense heat signature. She tapped the side of the goggles to revert to normal vision. Something about using voice commands around Lily felt silly.

"Woah," Lily murmured.

Shay agreed mentally. Even without thermal mode, the entire cave was visible because of light pouring from an opening about twenty yards away. They looked at each other and jogged toward the opening.

A large chamber lay beyond, bright as day but with no obvious light source. A white bed mat was arranged in the center, surrounded by soft cushions of different colors.

Shelves of polished obsidian adorned the walls of the chamber, each filled with colorful stones.

An obsidian pedestal held a beautiful blue-green ewer, elaborate patterns etched into the glass and threads of gold and silver crisscrossing it. It matched the description of the artifact perfectly.

Standing beside one of the shelves was a beautiful young Korean woman, her eyes as dark as night, and her hair in an elaborate series of braids held up with the help of gold and silver hairpins. Shay was no fashion expert on ancient Korea, but the woman's blue *hanbok* was consistent with some of the pictures she'd seen of the clothing from the Silla era.

The woman stepped forward, tilting her head. "Curious," she offered, her voice accented, but the words unmistakably English.

Shay exchanged a glance with Lily before returning her attention to the woman. "You speak English?"

The woman held out her hand, and a glowing white orb appeared. "Magic allows me to understand whatever tongue I need." She closed her hand, and the orb vanished. "You're foreigners. From far away." She frowned. "You are…Dutch?"

Shay snort-laughed before coughing. "Um, no. Not Dutch."

The woman nodded slowly. "Portuguese, then? You don't have the look of someone from Nifon."

Lily glanced at Shay, and she shook her head.

Huh. Judging by the clothes and the old-school name for Japan alone, this chick might have been out of circulation for a

*thousand years, but the Dutch and Portuguese shit makes me
think only a few hundred.*

"We're Americans," Shay explained.

The Korean woman pursed her lips in concentration. "Your country lies in Europe?"

Shay shrugged. "Farther west. The New World, some people might have called it when you last talked to them." She held up her hands. "I'm Shay." She nodded to Lily. "This is Lily."

The woman inhaled deeply. "This girl smells of magic. You have things that smell of magic, but she is a magical being."

Lily shrugged. "Sorry?"

The woman shook her head. "You can call me Aerye. I sleep so much now." She yawned. "It's hard to stay awake. It's been…so long. I have few visitors."

Shay frowned. "You can sleep when *dokkaebi* are wandering the cave?"

She's either lucky or much, much more than she appears.

Aerye nodded. "We have a mutually beneficial arrangement. Tell me, Shay and Lily of the Kingdom of America, why have you come here?"

Here goes nothing.

Shay cleared her throat. "I've come to recover the glass ewer of His Highness, King Bak Hyeokgeose."

Aerye's delicate eyebrows lifted. "Have you now?"

"I'm on an official mission from the Ministry of Culture, Sports, and Tourism of the Republic of Korea." Shay tried to sound as professional as she could.

The woman frowned. "Korea? I don't know this kingdom. I thought the Kingdom of Great Joseon laid claim to this area. Did perhaps the Goryeo rise again during my sleep?"

Shay shrugged. "I don't know when you last woke up, but a lot of things have changed. Hell, the Japan...um, even the people of Nifon ruled the area for a while, and now it's kind of split down the middle two competing, uh, kingdoms."

Aerye sniffed disdainfully. "It is the nature of humans to destroy themselves. You come for a blessed artifact from one of the few good humans to ever exist."

"I take it you're not human, then?"

The Korean woman shook her head. Nine glowing tails appeared behind her. "I am a *kumiho*. I have defended the ewer since the fall of Silla. I have no intention of turning it over to any new kingdom that claims dominion over the old lands. There was a reason I fled to this island."

Shay blinked. "Huh? I don't even get this. You're a *kumiho*, a nine-tailed shapeshifting fox, right? I don't know which legends are true, but your kind doesn't tend to care all that much about human politics, and what you said only confirms that. You care about guarding some artifact for an old king of a fallen kingdom?"

Lily stepped closer to Shay, her breathing slow.

Aerye shook her head. "There was a prince of the royal family of Silla. He was the owner, long after his ancestor. A glorious man, perfect in soul and body. His dying wish was that the enemies of his kingdom would not have his most treasured item. I swore to him that I would defend it, and I have for a thousand years." Her face darkened, and her eyes shifted from dark to orange with slit pupils. The glowing of her tails intensified, and sharp claws extended from her hands. "I don't care what kingdom you hail from or who you claim to serve. The ewer remains here."

Shay shook her head. "I've got no beef with you. I really don't want to have to hurt you."

Lily swallowed. "Shay, just got a really bad vision. We should...do something and fast."

The *kumiho* stared at the teen, inhaling deeply. "No. I can't let you leave. So much fresh blood on you. It's obvious you'll return with more and take what doesn't belong to you." She whipped her hand back and a ball of burning blue fire appeared, growing in size.

"Here we go again." Shay yanked out her pistol and opened fire. Lily joined her.

A bright blue flash caused each bullet to bounce to the ground, crushed.

Shay hissed. "I'll distract her this time. You try one of Tubal-Cain's little toys. She's a lot smaller than the *dokkaebi*."

The *kumiho* threw the blue fireball, and Shay and Lily jumped in opposite directions. The ball struck a wall, exploding in a shower of blue sparks.

Shay sprinted around the edge of the cave, firing a round every couple of seconds to keep Aerye focused on her. Her enemy kept hurling exploding blue fireballs, each narrowly missing.

Lily circled the opposite direction, pulling an adamantine knife from a sheath inside her jacket.

Shay emptied the rest of her magazine into the *kumiho*'s shield and pulled out her sword.

Aerye narrowed her eyes and took a step back.

Shay grinned. "You get it, don't you? This isn't an ordinary sword."

The *kumiho* slammed her palms together, and a wave of azure energy shot from her in all directions. Lily leapt over it, likely anticipating it with her abilities.

The magic blast slammed into Shay, knocking her onto her back. She managed to keep a grip on her sword but her stomach churned, and she regretted all the *banchan* and rice she'd had for breakfast.

Aerye ignored Lily behind her.

You shouldn't have been so sure she'd get hit, fox bitch.

The teen rushed straight toward the *kumiho* and slammed the knife into her back, and Aerye screamed and spun. A blade of blue light sprang from her wrist, and she came within a hairsbreadth of slicing Lily's throat before the teen somersaulted away.

Shay forced herself off the ground and ignored the pain and nausea to charge Aerye. The *kumiho* turned around just in time for the blade of the tachi to pierce her heart.

Aerye blinked several times and looked down at the crimson seeping from her wound. She coughed up some blood and gripped the blade. "I'm sorry, my prince. I've failed you."

Shay released her grip and Aerye fell backward, her tails vanishing but her claws and eyes remaining the same. With a final gasp, her head lolled to the side and her breathing stopped.

A moment later, Shay fell to her knees and clutched her stomach. "Oh, fuck. I don't feel great." She looked toward Lily. "You okay?"

Lily shrugged. "I think so. Are you seriously hurt? I don't see any new wound."

Shay managed to stand, her stomach still flipping but the discomfort starting to fade. "I've been better, but I think I'll live." She shook her head and looked down at the dead *kumiho*. "Shit. It didn't have to go down that way. This was supposed to be a nice aboveboard legal recovery job."

Lily knelt over Aerye and closed her eyes. "She guarded the ewer for a thousand years for some guy who died before our country even existed. That's devotion."

Shay snorted. "Maybe, or maybe it's delusion and obsession. I'm not sitting around in a cave for a thousand years guarding anything." She rolled her eyes. "With my luck, James would want me to guard his stupid truck for that long."

She headed toward the pedestal and looked over her shoulder. "Don't worry, Aerye. At least this isn't going to be sold to some asshole for a private collection. The Korean people will benefit from it, and at least some are probably descendants of the man you loved so much."

Devotion and love. Hell, love is still a weird idea for me. What would it be like to spend the rest of my life with James?

Her eyes widened and her cheeks heated.

Lily looked at Shay, curiosity on her face "Something wrong?"

Shay waved a hand dismissively. "Just some aftereffects of her spell."

The rest of my life, huh?

James picked up the phone and dialed Alison. He was surprised she hadn't called him. For all he knew, she was also monitoring all big crime news in Los Angeles for Brownstone-related incidents.

"Hey, Dad," she answered cheerfully. "What's up?"

He rubbed the back of his neck and grunted. "Just figured I should be honest with you."

"About what?"

James frowned. "You didn't hear about it on the news?"

"I've been busy. Classes and…well, a lot of stuff. It's a magic school, you know." Alison chuckled. It sounded a bit nervous to James.

Probably boy shit. I get it, Shay. I have to let her grow up. I won't ask.

At least that was what he told himself. He couldn't be sure if it was that or more that he didn't want to get into an argument about secrets.

"Some guys tried to come after me," James explained. "It wasn't a big deal. Well, they *did* damage a barbeque restaurant, but no one got hurt. Except for them. They're all dead. But they had it coming. I wanted to tell you about it before you heard shit on the news."

He grunted, worrying about his language. During the summer they'd spent training together and going out on bounty hunts, he'd fallen out of the habit of controlling himself around Alison. It seemed kind of silly to worry about a few bad words when his daughter was helping him take down dangerous criminals.

If she can beat down witches, she can hear a few shits and fucks.

Alison groaned. "Is Mom there?"

"She's in Korea on a tomb raid, but she completed it, and she'll be back tomorrow."

The girl let out a sigh of relief. "Just try not to do anything crazy until she comes back."

"Crazy like what?"

"Oh, I don't know, maybe attacking an entire building like you did with the Harriken."

James grunted. "Hey, they kept at me until I had no choice."

Alison snorted. "No attacking buildings filled with bad guys without at least some people backing you up. If not Mom, then the guys at the agency. Promise me."

"Fine," James grumbled. "I promise not to attack any buildings filled with bad guys without backup."

A merry laugh followed. "That's all I wanted. I love you, Dad. Be careful, and remember you always have the wish if you need it."

"I love you, too."

Fuck using the wish. That's hers, and it'll stay hers.

Trey, Max, and six more Brownstone bounty hunters surrounded the target house.

Too easy. Why hasn't this fucker taken a shot? This was near the top of the list that hacker chick gave us.

Trey shook his head. A dangerous target was inside, a wizard who called himself the VR King on the dark web. When Heather had sent Trey the list, she'd warned him there were some oddities about the VR King's online presence, and she wouldn't be surprised if he had used magic to alter or scrub some of it. That might explain why VR King only had a level-one bounty for draining a few bank accounts despite being a self-admitted wizard specializing in fire and electronic magic, yet another detail linking him to the attack on James.

They'd shown up for one important reason. The VR King had been bragging lately about how he was ready to move up in the world and "kill himself a pussy-ass mother-fucker like James Brownstone."

Every Brownstone Agency bounty hunter present was suited up with armor, assault rifles, and anti-magic deflectors. They lacked the trademark Brownstone Agency suits and looked more like an AET team.

Trey nodded to Max, who stood on the corner. He signaled the next man. They didn't want to risk using phones. They couldn't be sure if the VR King would be able to detect the calls.

Lachlan moved up to the front door, shotgun loaded with a breaching round and racked, and indicated that he was ready.

Trey held up three fingers, then two, then one.

The shotgun spewed out its cargo, blowing through the lock. Lachlan rolled to the side as Trey charged in to knock the door open, his rifle ready. He stepped to the side and swept the room. Another man entered, then another.

"Living room clear," Trey shouted.

"Kitchen clear," Manuel yelled from the other side of the house.

No problem entering front or back. This shit was too easy.

Trey gritted his teeth. No way the VR King could be taken down this easily. That was when he heard it.

Someone shouting from a room down the hall.

Trey rushed forward, his rifle still at the ready. Lachlan and Carl fell in behind him. They continued running until they found the source of the shouting, another closed door.

Lachlan and Carl fanned out to either side of Trey. The senior bounty hunter took a deep breath and kicked open the door.

"Repeat myself?" shouted a voice from the darkened room inside. "I said you should kill yourself, you dumbass pussy noob motherfucker. If that doesn't happen, maybe get cancer while I'm riding your mom. That's what you get for fucking with the VR King."

A soft glow came from the side of the room. Someone encased in a thick VR headset, gloves, and headphones sat in front of a computer. Something was wrong.

Too fucking small. Is the VR King a gnome or a dwarf or some shit like that? Not a wizard?

Trey kept his gun trained on the person in front of the computer and flipped on the room light.

"You've got to be fucking kidding me," he muttered.

The person encased in nothing but his boxers and VR gear wasn't a dangerous wizard or an Oriceran, but a human kid, probably twelve or thirteen at most.

Trey shouldered his rifle and walked over to the computer. Apparently, their dangerous bounty was playing some sort of VR shooting game.

Several more bounty hunters made it into the room and the men spread out, shouldering their rifles and watching. The rest waited in the hall.

Judging by the screen, the VR King was running

81

through a virtual corridor of an Oriceran castle shooting various Kilomea and elves with a simulated rifle.

"Yeah, suck on it," the kid yelled. "You can't fucking handle this heat. You are all a bunch of whiny mother-fucking bitches who couldn't get a positive KDA if your whore mother offered to blow you over it. You think I'm a kid using a voice modulator? You wish I was, you dumbass piece-of-shit cocksucker dog-fucker. I'm a fucking night-mare. I'm fucking you up the ass right now, and you don't even know it. Maybe I'll use a spell, trace your ass, and then fireball you for fucking questioning me, you non-magical bitch."

Trey whistled. "Damn! That boy's got a mouth. I don't know if I'm old enough to hear this."

The rest of the bounty hunters laughed.

"What the fuck are you talking about?" the VR King shouted. "No one is in the room with me. You're just hearing shit. I told you, I play this shit using magic from Oriceran because humans are nothing but pussy bitches. I do this to help me train. I'm gonna fuck up people next in real life. AET. James Brownstone. Those cocksucking motherfuckers are gonna cry when the VR King comes for them."

Trey shook his head and marched over to the boy, yanked off the headset, and tossed it on the desk.

"What the fuck, Mom?" the VR King screamed. "I told you never to do that shit." He spun toward Trey and all the color drained from his face. "Uh, who are you?"

All the anger and feigned street accent left the boy's voice.

Trey crossed his arms. "You're the VR King? The guy with a level-one bounty?"

The boy laughed nervously. "Look, that wasn't even me. I read about it on some message board, and I just took credit for it. Oh shit. You're the cops? You're AET, aren't you?"

Trey shook his head. "We're with the Brownstone Agency. We heard that a wizard named the VR King was threatening to kill our boss, so we decided to go catch his ass first."

The VR King groaned and lowered his head. "It's all just shit-talking. Psych warfare, you know? If people think I'm a badass wizard in real life, they don't play as well, and I do better against them. Besides, kill James Brownstone?" The kid laughed, the confidence and street accent returning. "I don't think a fucking army of zombie dragons could kill James Motherfucking Brownstone."

The men all chuckled, and Trey nodded.

"Ain't no point in bringing in a kid who ain't even the bounty. Next time, pick some other guy to threaten." Trey shrugged. "We ain't paying for the door, though."

The kid winced. "Man, my mom will freak. She's going to take my computer away."

Trey laughed and shook his head. "Let's go, boys. If this is how this shit starts, we're gonna have to run down a *lot* of leads."

CHAPTER EIGHT

S hay laughed, from the other side of the couch. "So far your investigation has netted a bunch of wannabes and one foul-mouthed pre-teen?"

James grunted.

Shit, I'm glad she's back, but I don't know who I want more: worried Shay or mocking Shay.

"The guys are chasing down leads from Heather."

"Peyton's still on vacation, but I can make him work remotely."

James shook his head. "It's fine. I've also got Tyler working the underworld angle more directly." He shrugged. "And there might not be shit to find. Those four guys I killed might have been it."

Shay snorted. "Bullshit. Whenever people start taking shots at you, it never stops with the first few idiots." She frowned. "This shit's gonna escalate. As fun as fake wizards are, there are real people out there who want you dead. I wouldn't be surprised if the first guys were just to feel you out. You should be considering getting out of town for a few weeks until we can chase this all down."

"No fucking way. I'm not afraid of those assholes. If they have to test me, then they don't have what it takes to kill me. So fuck them. I'll kill every one of the bastards who comes at me." He scoffed.

Shay rolled her eyes. "It'll be really inconvenient if someone blows your house up again, and if you have to live at my place, keep in mind it's gonna be my rules, not your OCD KISS Brownstone shit."

James scrubbed a hand over his face. "Fuck. I should issue a public challenge. Just get them to come at me all at once. Tyler can even make some money off it."

"No." Shay slapped her hands on her hips. "No fucking way. We're not gonna give up any shit to anyone until we know who we're dealing with. For all you know, the minute you do that, you give them some special spell focus they can use to melt your balls." She leaned forward. "Not only that, but they already didn't mind going after you in public. If you issue a public challenge, they might not let you pick a dried-up lakebed. They might just decide to come after you in the middle of LA. You ever think about that?"

James frowned. "Then I'll just wait until Tyler and Heather turn something up." He leaned back against the couch. "I'm annoyed at all this shit. It's so fucking complicated. How many asses do I need to kick before people understand they don't fucking come after me?"

Tyler took a breath and slowly stood, staring down at the message on his computer.

No, no, no. I don't want to have to go there again. Not so soon.

A light knock came from his office door.

"Come in."

Kathy stepped in, a slight smirk on her face. "You going to hide back here all night, Tyler?"

He frowned. "I'm not hiding. I'm looking into this Brownstone hit."

The smirk vanished, overwritten by curiosity. "Any luck?"

Tyler blew out a breath. "The few things I've found make me think this isn't over, and this is a lot more hard-core magic than anyone realizes." He ran a hand through his hair. "I'm going to have to hit some magical contacts."

Kathy closed the door, crossed her arms, and leaned against the wall. "So? Dannec doesn't even charge you that much, all things considered."

"If only it were that easy." He shook his head. "Fuck, from what I've found out these guys are linked to serious dark magic. Dannec won't cut it. I'm going to have to go to the Eyes."

Kathy snickered. "That thing or guy or whatever the hell he is redefines 'creepy as fuck.'" She shook her head. "You're gonna end up dead if you keep sticking your nose into things you don't understand."

Tyler scoffed. "That's what being an information broker is. No way you can reach the top if you're afraid of a few... weird contacts." He narrowed his eyes. "You know what. *You* should go talk to the Eyes."

She paled. "What?"

He pointed at her. "You're always talking about how you want to up your game. Well, time to put on your big-girl panties and prove it. If you want to be more than a third-rate backup for me, you'll need to learn to deal with guys like the Eyes."

Kathy swallowed and forced a grin onto her face. "Sure. Bring it on. If the guy hasn't eaten you yet, he'll love *me*."

Tyler smirked. "Keep in mind that whatever he is, he's not human, so being a hot brunette isn't going to mean shit."

Kathy winked. "Don't worry, I've got a lot more assets than a nice pair of tits and a great ass." She stepped out of the room and slammed the door too hard.

More nervous than you're letting on? Good. You shouldn't be relaxed around the Eyes. It's safer that way.

Tyler fell back into his chair and shook his head. It'd be a good test, and he needed to make better use of the beautiful and intelligent woman anyway.

Brownstone's got a whole fucking army working under him now. I've been so greedy that I've been too afraid to hire another bartender, and I fired all the waitresses.

He shook his head. Losing to Brownstone in ass-kicking or intimidation was one thing, but some things weren't acceptable.

Tyler slammed his fist on the desk. "There's no damned way I can let Brownstone be a better businessman than me."

James wandered down the sidewalk several blocks from his house. Every once in a while, someone would pass him in a car and give him a wave or a nod.

He chuckled. Although he'd hosted several community barbeque events, it was rare that he walked around his neighborhood. He wasn't sure if people were more or less comfortable with the famous James Brownstone after those.

Community outreach wasn't his goal, though. Ever since he'd almost hit the dog, he hadn't been able to get it out of his mind. Was the dog a pet? A stray? Some rich family's dog who had gotten lost and was far from home?

James grunted.

Rich family? Shit. I could buy up most of this neighborhood. I keep telling myself I'm not some rich asshole, but I could stop bounty hunting right now and not know how to spend all the money I already have.

He patted his chest. The last thing he wanted to do was have a major fight in his neighborhood, but if any trouble looked like it was coming, he could bond with the amulet in seconds.

Shit. Maybe I should just be bonded to Whispy all the time.

No, that was a terrible idea. He narrowed his eyes. Maybe the only reason he was still in control was that he didn't keep himself constantly connected to the amulet. What would it be like to have Whispy Doom in his head all the time? The damned amulet could nag him into submission if anything could.

James kept moving. He needed to find the dog. Once he did, he could get it out of his head, and it'd be one less thing distracting him. One less thing making his life more complicated.

The seconds stretched into minutes, and then into an hour before he finally caught sight of familiar dark fur in an alley behind a convenience store. James charged toward the alley.

A couple coming out of the grocery store yelped and hurried back inside.

Shit. I'm not going after a bounty, people.

This time he got a good look at the dog. Dark, short, flat coat and floppy ears, good size, probably over sixty pounds. James wasn't an expert, but he'd read enough websites on dogs when he'd first gotten Leeroy to have memorized many breeds. If he had to guess, he'd say the dog was a mix of a Labrador Retriever and Weimaraner. That made the dog a so-called Labmaraner.

He wasn't sure if some people would consider the dog a designer breed or just a mutt.

The dog zipped down the alley before he could get close to it. James picked up the pace, but despite all his gifts, an impressive sprinting speed wasn't one of them.

He reached the end of the alley and looked both ways down the street. No sign of the dog.

"Fuck. Why is the dog running? Oh, because some huge tattooed asshole is chasing him." James let out a loud groan and scrubbed his face with his hand.

There's got to be a better way to find that dog.

CHAPTER NINE

Kathy tried to steady her hands as she stepped up to the fearsome Kilomea guarding the double doors to the Eyes' converted warehouse.

Purple suit and gold chains? Tyler wasn't kidding. The guy really does look like an ogre pimp.

The Kilomea silently stared down at Kathy, curling and uncurling his meaty hands.

Yeah, I get it. You're super-intimidating.

"I'm here to see the Eyes," she managed to say without a single squeak. "On behalf of Tyler."

The Kilomea sneered. "What? He piss himself last time he was here, so he sends you?"

Kathy shrugged. "Something like that. Maybe."

The bouncer snickered and threw open the doors. "You know where to go?"

She nodded quickly.

"Then fucking hurry. I'm only letting you in because my

boss says he's taking a liking to Tyler." The Kilomea gave her a toothy grin. "Maybe someday he'll take his soul."

He's just trying to fuck with you. Don't react.

Kathy shrugged. "That sounds…interesting, but I should really talk to him. Time-sensitive matter."

She managed a grin and stepped through the doors. They slammed shut behind her, and she sighed deeply. A second later, she coughed on the thick smoke in the air and shook her head, hurrying straight down the hallway and doing her best to ignore all the people lying about, not dead, but their minds elsewhere, the flicker of magic around them.

Always got to find a new way to get high. That's humanity for you.

When Kathy arrived at her destination, another set of double doors, she was surprised by the presence of two gnomes. Tyler had told her to expect an elf and a human guard.

One of the gnomes eyed her with obvious disdain.

Wonder what a gnome is looking for in a hot woman? Probably not someone taller than him.

"What?" the gnome barked.

Kathy straightened her back to project confidence. "I'm here to see the Eyes on behalf of Tyler."

The gnomes exchanged glances, and the first one knocked once. He held out his hand. "Your purse. Or you can just give us the gun inside it."

Kathy snorted and handed the gnome her purse.

The gnome sneered. "Enjoy your visit, *Miss.*"

Annoyance outweighed her fear, and she rolled her eyes.

Fuck you. Men are fucking annoying whether they are tall or short.

The gnome opened one of the doors.

Kathy stepped inside the dimly lit and empty room and took several deep breaths as the gnome slammed the door shut. She waved her hand to try to push some of the smoke out of her face.

She sensed them before she worked up the courage to turn toward them, the two solid-yellow glowing eyes not attached to a body. She blinked, and for a second she thought she could make out the vague outline of a shape beneath and around them, but it was gone as soon as she concentrated.

"Now Tyler sends his underlings," the Eyes offered in a voice barely above a whisper. "Does he fear me so much, Kathy?"

The Eyes already knows my name? I didn't even tell that asshole at the front.

Kathy shrugged. "Probably."

"Do you?"

She considered lying for a second, but there didn't seem to be a point. "Yes."

A wheezing laugh followed. "Why?"

Kathy shrugged. "Because I don't know what the fuck you are, so I can't even *begin* to figure out how to deal with you."

The creature jumped to another shadowy corner in an instant. "What *do* you know, then? This is your one chance to impress me. The only reason I do business with Tyler is that he impressed me at our first meeting. If you fail, you will leave this place with nothing. If you fail severely, you won't leave this place at all."

She swallowed, her heart thundering. Her first instinct was to yell he couldn't get away with killing her and that Tyler knew where she was, but she didn't voice the thought. The Eyes killed all sorts of people and got away with it.

"You have a body," she blurted. "Even though it's hard to see. I think it's right where we'd think it should be, however weird it might look."

"Why do you say that?"

Kathy forced her most triumphant grin onto her face. "Pure observation."

The glowing yellow orbs wandered from the shadows until they stared right into Kathy's eyes from inches away. "Explain your observation, little girl."

Kathy took a deep breath and slipped her hands into her pockets so he couldn't see them shaking. "This place. It's too secure if you're the ghost you want to pretend you are. Why the big bouncer?"

The Eyes let out another wheezing laugh. "That's it? That's your great proof? I have clients who are indisposed and not capable of protecting themselves. Security is necessary for *their* benefit, not mine."

"Bullshit," Kathy shouted. She winced.

Fuck, fuck, fuck. I'm not dealing with Tyler here. I need to watch my mouth.

He moved closer until his yellow eyes were so close they were almost touching hers. A biting chill stabbed Kathy's face, and she grimaced and forced her own eyes to stay open.

"Explain," the creature demanded. "Choose your next words carefully. If they are wrong, you die right here, right now."

Kathy managed to keep her body from trembling, even though every instinct in every cell screamed for her to turn and run from the monster in front of her. "The Kilomea might be there to protect your guests, but you have guards in front of your room; guards who disarm people." She shook her head, her heart still pounding but her confidence building. "That doesn't make sense if you're a bodiless demon. If you were immune to guns, you wouldn't care. You'd let someone shoot you and laugh in their face, and you don't have the Kilomea take the guns, so you're less concerned about someone shooting a guest than you claim." She shrugged. "Not saying someone could take you out with a single shot, but obviously you *can* be shot. You can probably bleed."

The Eyes backed up several feet and took his chill with him. "A deception, perhaps."

Kathy shook her head. "You like being theatrical. It'd make more sense for you to let someone try to shoot you. I don't know why we can't see your body, if it's naturally like that or it's a spell, but I do know if say, James Brownstone came here and decided to kick your ass, you might be in trouble. Even the Eyes can know fear."

Complete silence gripped the room. Kathy's heart beat harder as the seconds ticked away.

The Eyes' barking laugh turned into a wheeze. "You impress me, little girl. Let's talk about your threat—your Brownstone. That's why you're here, isn't it?"

Kathy nodded quickly. "Someone's trying to kill him. He wants to know who."

"What will you give me for this information?"

She shrugged. "What do you want?"

He winked back into the original shadowy corner where she'd first spotted his eyes. "Will you give me anything I ask?"

"I might be inexperienced, but I'm not a fucking moron. There's no way I'll give you *anything* you want."

"Clever girl." The Eyes chuckled. "A freebie, to welcome you to your new world. Next time, it'll cost a lot more, and there may be a test."

Kathy narrowed her eyes. "A test?"

"I see...potential in you. Younger, more flexible in mind. Brave. Braver than Tyler. Sharper. His mind sees only money. Your hunger is different, deeper. More fundamental."

She couldn't stop the tremors of revulsion that passed through her. "Okay, then. We can...talk about different tests and projects in the future, but what about the information I came for?"

"One left," the Eyes wheezed. "One left from the Council. Not a traitor, but not really one of them. He Who Hunts. He craves more now, and Brownstone is the key to something grand...awful or good, I can't say, but grand. He's sent men."

Kathy looked down for a moment and nodded. "Where is this...thing hiding?"

"I won't tell you."

"Can't or won't."

The Eyes disappeared. "Maybe both," he whispered into her face.

Her skin crawled. "Is there anything else about it?"

"Brownstone has already felt their touch. Others have as well. Look for the signs. Look for the tunnels."

Kathy stepped back toward the door, sensing she wasn't going to get much more and wanting to get far, far away from the Eyes and take a shower. "Thank you."

When she turned around, she found the glowing yellow eyes right front of her. She hissed in surprise.

"I'll be watching," the Eyes whispered. "Watching to see if you're worth my further attention."

He disappeared again and Kathy rushed for the double doors, throwing both open, snatching her purse from the gnome and running down the hall.

Heather tapped on her keyboard, trying to narrow down possible locations. From what James had passed along to her, he was being targeted by the last remnants of the Council and their base of operations might be associated with tunnels somehow.

She sighed and shook her head. It wasn't exactly like Los Angeles had a shortage of tunnels.

A click of the mouse brought up a window filled with search query hits, a mix of unusual sightings associated with either tunnels or anything near tunnels.

Heather narrowed her eyes and clicked on the third entry on her list with a frown.

"Strange sightings near abandoned subway tunnels," she murmured. "On the same day James was attacked."

On a hunch, Heather clicked to another window, a missing person database. She performed a search for Los Angeles County starting the day of James' attack. She then checked the same time interval before the day of James' attack.

A pretty big uptick. Why hasn't this been in the news?

Heather scanned the list and ran searches on some of the missing people. The pattern became clear quickly: runaways, prostitutes, and street people for the most part. The kinds of victims that a city was willing to ignore or at least not pay special attention to.

Her stomach twisted, and she sucked in a breath. She wasn't naïve enough to believe any of those people were still alive.

If I correlate the missing person reports with the subway tunnel sightings, I can probably narrow down the location and get James a search area at least.

Heather took a deep breath and slapped her cheeks. If the missing people were victims of the last remnants of the Council, it might be too late to save them, but it wasn't too late to get revenge for them.

James grunted into his phone as he stood in his kitchen. "Thanks, Heather. Sounds like you've got a good general location. Maybe prep some drones for recon, but don't send any into the tunnels yet. I'll talk to you soon." He ended the call and slipped his phone back into his pocket.

Shay watched him from the dining room chair, her arms crossed. "What's the word?"

"From what Heather could find, the assholes still have guys in town, and they're probably killing innocent people in abandoned subway tunnels." James frowned. "Fuckers. I knew I should have issued a public challenge. They're killing people every day I don't finish him off, and we still only have a general fucking area. Even if I get all the guys, who knows how long it'll take to search those damned tunnels? Heather could only narrow it down so much."

Shay shook her head. "First of all, this shit isn't your fault. It's this He Who Hunts asshole and his lackeys. Second, I know how we can figure out his location very precisely."

James frowned. "What? Call Peyton in? What's he gonna do that Heather hasn't already?"

She shook her head. "Nope. You keep forgetting that I happen to know a whole swarm of magical teenagers who know the tunnels of Los Angeles better than anyone. I guarantee that if I call Harry and feed him the information Heather gave you, we will know exactly where to go within hours."

"You think so?"

Shay nodded. "I damned well *know* so. The only question is, what's our next move once we know?"

James grunted. "It's time for me to stop fucking sitting around and do what I do best. I'll get the guys together, and we'll march down there and fucking waste every single Council sonofabitch we run into. We'll find that He Who Hunts asshole and slice him into so many pieces, you'll need a microscope to find one." He slammed his fist on the counter. "These fuckers killed Shorty, and now they have the balls to come back? You make your call. I'm gonna call Trey and tell him to bring everyone in. Once we know where to go, we'll march there, and I'll show them why the Harriken and the Nuevo Gulf Cartel no longer exist." He snorted. "And I don't even have to break any promises to Alison."

"What promises?" Shay arched a brow.

"I promised not to attack any buildings filled with bad guys without backup. Preferably you." James shrugged.

Shay grinned. "Aww, the family that slays together stays together." She winked. "I'll call Harry. Time to make 'He Who Hunts' into 'He Who Cries Like a Little Bitch.'"

CHAPTER TEN

The heavy thud of dozens of men in boots echoed in the darkened tunnels, their head and wrist lamps cutting through the darkness. Every Brownstone Agency bounty hunter in the city had been called for the raid. They didn't have time to wait for reinforcements from Vegas. Trey marched at the front of the bounty hunter formation but behind Shay and James.

This was war, and again the men resembled soldiers more than bounty hunters in their helmets, dark tactical gear, and anti-magic deflectors. Style wasn't necessary when they were on a mission of extermination.

Many of them were grim-faced, undoubtedly thinking of their fallen friend. Most of them hadn't been able to participate in any of James' follow-up raids. It was their time to give a little payback.

They'd finish off some sadistic bastards and pick up a paycheck from the government. It was about to be a very good day.

Shay had been right. Harry and his friends had given her the location within an hour. One of them almost got zapped by a wizard and had barely managed to escape.

James wasn't worried about the Council forces fleeing. Harry and his friends were watching the outer perimeter, and they hadn't seen anything except when they'd gotten too close.

Whispy Doom radiated excitement in James' mind, offering only the occasional murmur about killing the enemy. The damned thing wouldn't shut up when he was sitting around but could be as a quiet as an altar boy in church if it knew James was on the way to destroy people.

The bounty hunters murmured amongst themselves.

Shay walked alongside James. "These Council guys are kind of fucking morons."

James grunted. "Why do you say that?"

"It was one thing when we were hitting them at their base or one of their safehouses, but they've come onto your turf." She shrugged. "And they only have one true Council member left."

"The Harriken didn't know when to stop either." James frowned. "The only problem is, I can't blow up all those tunnels like I did their headquarters."

Shay laughed. "You don't always have to blow everything up."

He shrugged. "When I did it to the Harriken, they stopped coming back. Didn't do it to the Council, and I still have to deal with them."

"A good point. Next time we bring a bomb." Shay patted the hilt of her sword. "Would you have gotten involved if they'd never kidnapped me?"

James furrowed his brow and thought that over for a moment. "Don't know. Lot of good money in level-six bounties."

"Not that you need it." She grinned.

"I have a feeling the fuckers would have pissed me off sooner or later." James shrugged and turned his head to call to his men, "Two more rights and we should run right into them. Remember, this is still an official dead-or-alive organizational bounty. If they don't immediately surrender, fucking waste them."

The gathered men nodded.

Trey turned to the others. "Go ahead and load your anti-magic bullets. We know these bitches are mostly gonna be wizards." He pulled a magazine out of his tactical vest and slapped it into his rifle. "And remember—this is for Shorty."

"For Shorty!" the men shouted in unison.

Shay sighed and shook her head. "So much for the element of surprise."

James grunted. "Fuck surprise. I want those bitches to know we're coming."

Insufficient power for advanced transformation, his amulet whispered.

We don't need that shit yet.

Tactical potential not reached. Consider implications of allied forces.

James glanced down at his covered chest. That wasn't a line Whispy Doom had used before. Was the amulet trying to convince him a different way?

It didn't matter. He didn't know what the situation was supposed to be, but for now, he was the one who called the shots, and Whispy Doom could fucking deal.

"Let's do this shit," James shouted and broke into a sprint.

The men rushed after him, their rifles ready. When they hit the first intersection, light shone from down the tunnel.

Makes sense. Not like wizards can see in the dark automatically.

James picked up the pace. At this point, he doubted the Council could throw anything at him his amulet hadn't already encountered. He turned at the next intersection.

A line of wizards flanked by strange monsters waited, their wands up. A man with rock skin stood to the side. At least nine other men looked identical except for different-colored glowing eyes. A giant spider with the head of a man crouched in the back. A human torso was connected to four pointed legs and a long serpentine tail. A few other nightmarish creatures stood ready.

What the fuck is all this?

New enemies, Whispy Doom sent. *Kill enemies. Adapt. Grow stronger.*

James didn't have more than a few seconds to ponder the unholy horrors standing in front of him before the wizards opened fire, a volley of elemental forces exploding around him. He gritted his teeth and stumbled back, the combined blast stinging more than he'd expected.

Near maximum adaptation potential presented. Kill enemies. Find new, stronger enemies. Adapt.

Shay and the men behind him held their breaths, waiting for the smoke and dust to clear. Even the Council forces watched in breathless silence. Everyone seemed to realize the true threat in the area.

James smirked and wiped a small trickle of blood off his face. He had a few minor cuts and reddened skin. His clothes were shredded, his shirt almost gone, but he didn't care anymore if anyone saw the amulet. Even if they didn't need to know he was an alien, he had no problem with them knowing he had a special artifact he used during jobs. Like most people, they would just assume it was magical.

He advanced and shrugged. "You get one fucking chance. Drop to your knees right now, or we end you fuckers." He looked around with a frown. "And where the fuck is He Who Hunts?"

The wizards responded with another blinding barrage. Stone, dirt, concrete, and metal blasted in the air, raining down in the chamber.

James opened fire at the closest wizard, his anti-magic bullets cutting through the man's second-rate shield. The guy jerked and spun, doing a final dance of death.

The Brownstone men all opened fire now, as did Shay. Half of the wizards and glowing-eyed clones lay on the ground dead or dying before the Council troops realized their mistake in concentrating on James and believing their defenses would protect them from small-arms fire.

The remaining wizards hurriedly backed up while the mutants and monsters advanced. The anti-magic bullets bounced off the rock-skinned man with a spark, and he grinned and charged.

James grunted and holstered his pistol as he rushed the man. They slammed into each other, the loud thud booming like a thunderclap in the tunnel. The rock man's eyes widened, and he staggered back from the force of the blow. The bounty hunter grunted, barely feeling the impact.

He cracked his knuckles. "You can ask my girlfriend how hard a head I have, asshole." He threw another punch and slammed a fist into the rock man, whose head snapped back.

James shook out his hand. The man didn't just *look* like a rock, he *felt* like one. If he hadn't been using Whispy Doom, he might have broken his hand.

The two exchanged blows, but it was obvious that despite the rock man's magical armor, he lacked the bounty hunter's natural strength. Punch after punch sent the mutant stumbling back, cracks appearing in his face and chest and pieces of rock flying off him.

Kill enemy and find stronger enemy, Whispy Doom demanded. *Current enemy defensive abilities insufficient to promote additional adaptation.*

The loud echoes of gunfire continued as the Brownstone army downed wizards and monsters. A fireball exploded near the line, and several men yelled out in pain. A blue ray blasted from one wizard's wand, nailing Max in the shoulder. The bounty hunter fell to the ground, grimacing in pain, his anti-magic deflector dark but still intact.

Shay had already pulled her sword and now charged toward the mutant with the serpent tail. Her enemy snapped his tail at her and she leapt into the air, avoiding the blow. She landed in an expert roll and was on her feet again, all her momentum preserved. With a quick slash, she beheaded her enemy and didn't even stop to watch his head roll away as she charged the spider mutant.

James threw another series of vicious punches into the rock man's face, and his foe stumbled, dazed. The bounty hunter took his opportunity to grab the man's neck and yanked him to the ground. The mutant groaned, but James didn't let up as he slammed his face into the hard concrete.

"Rock and a hard place, asshole."

Insufficient energy for advanced transformation, Whispy Doom complained.

James ignored his needy symbiotic partner and the roar of gunfire and exploding magic around him as he continued to slam the rock man's head into the concrete. After his sixth hit, the entire head cracked and split in two. No blood came out, and the inside was nothing except rock and dust.

How the fuck does that even work? Damned magic.

He stood and dusted his hands off just in time to see Shay slice through a leg of the spider mutant. It took him a few seconds to realize she'd already cut several off. With a grin, she stabbed at the monster's body as it thrashed until it rolled onto its back and stopped moving.

Find new enemies. Kill. Adapt to become stronger.

James swept his head around, looking for more ass to kick. Dead wizards, clones, mutants, and monsters littered the floor. A few of his men lay against the wall, bloodstains on their armor, but they all were well enough to down healing potions.

He grunted and frowned. "Where's He Who Hunts?"

Trey jogged over from the corner. He didn't look wounded, but there was a huge claw mark scoring his armor. "Didn't see any motherfucker who looked like that dude. I don't think he was here, big man."

"Maybe he never was." James shrugged. "Just a bunch of dead-enders. The military wounded that fucker before he ran anyway. He probably bled out, and these assholes just came to avenge him. Probably his dying wish or some shit."

"What about what Tyler said?"

James shook his head. "He's not always right, and he said this was their base of operations. If the Council's guy is such a badass and still alive, why would he let me keep fucking his guys up? Nah. He's fucking dead already. I'd bet you money."

He stared down at one of the dead mutants or whatever the hell they were. No. Everything was over. This had to be the big plan, to ambush him with a bunch of wizards and monsters.

Shay wandered toward the pair after cleaning her sword on the shirt of a dead wizard. "They weren't surprised to see us, but I don't think they thought we'd show up with everyone."

Trey snorted. "Now these fuckers are dead." He pounded his chest. "For you, Shorty."

The other men cheered. "For Shorty!"

Max limped over, a healing potion in hand. His leg had been badly burned. He downed the potion and grinned. "Good thing we got all these fucking healing potions."

"Yeah," Lachlan called. "Good thing the big man can buy 'em in bulk at a discount because of Trey the Gigolo."

Shay laughed. "Trey the Gigolo?"

James grunted. He knew Trey had been seeing Zoe, and even though he couldn't understand why a man would take that kind of risk, the last thing he was going to do is tell any man who he should sleep with.

Trey frowned. "Y'all shut the fuck up. Y'all just jealous because you ain't have a girlfriend as fine as mine."

The men all laughed. James cracked a smile too, even if he disagreed. Zoe was nice, but she was no Shay.

Inefficient use of time, Whispy Doom all but shouted in James' mind. *Minimal adaptation gained from engaging enemies.*

It's my fucking time to waste. I don't fight people just to get stronger.

Inefficient.

I've been called worse, asshole.

Asshole is incorrect designation.

James surveyed the carnage and nodded, satisfied. Tyler, Heather, and Harry's information had pointed him there. If there were some other secret part of LA where He Who Hunts was still around, they would have found it. The bastard had to be dead.

We've won. This shit is finally over.

He Who Hunts floated back and forth. The scrying windows allowed him a perfect view of the battle, but his excitement had quickly turned to disappointment.

The loss of his forces was irrelevant. The wizards, transformed or otherwise, were nothing but disposable tools. They were there only to serve their purpose. The changed ones wouldn't last long anyway. The real problem came with what hadn't happened.

Brownstone had never transformed. It was obvious from the first attack that the bounty hunter hadn't used whatever artifact strengthened him and produced his powerful suit. In the second attack, his ability to take so many direct blasts proved he *was* using his artifact, but he hadn't transformed. No armor, no helmet, no green rays of destruction.

This would not do. Controlling Brownstone would require the man to be at his maximum potential, which was associated with the rage and anger He Who Hunts had tasted earlier. The red crystal would require it.

He Who Hunts glided over to an open door leading to another room. He had to be careful. Attacking Brownstone with serious force would be the best way to pull out his true nature, but it risked bringing the government to reinforce the man. If he couldn't corrupt Brownstone before the government got involved, he'd be forced to leave Earth for a while. All his time with the Council, all the corrupt threads he'd woven through Earth—everything could be wasted.

Brownstone couldn't be left behind. He was too useful a tool of chaos and death. He'd slaughtered hundreds of men in a mad quest to avenge a mere beast.

Insofar as He Who Hunts could feel affection, he was starting to like James Brownstone.

He Who Hunts floated into another room. Dozens of people lay on the ground, their hands and feet bound with glowing red magical thread.

"Please," a man cried. "I just want to go home."

More sobs and pleas came in a half-dozen languages. It'd been risky grabbing raw materials from all over the Earth. He Who Hunts could never be sure if the PDA or other such groups would be able to track him, but harvesting all of the necessary raw materials from Los Angeles wasn't practical. For now, he had enough for the next phase in his plan.

"You should rejoice," he rasped, his voice hollow and cold. "You are about to be repurposed into something far more useful."

CHAPTER ELEVEN

An insistent knock came from James' front door.

Shay frowned. "Who the fuck is that?"

James rose from the couch and headed toward the door. "Someone I've been expecting."

Something wasn't sitting right with Shay about the raid a few days prior. The government had paid the bounty. They also admitted they'd not seen so much as a single red particle of He Who Hunts, but it was hard for her to believe the creature was dead, even though James seemed certain.

Am I just looking for reasons to be paranoid, or is he looking for reasons to pretend everything's okay?

James opened the door to reveal a pack of tween children.

Shay blinked. That was about the last thing she expected.

James reached into his pocket to pull out his wallet and

fish out a few large bills. He handed one to each of the kids. "Find anything?"

Okay, that explains why he's carried so much cash on him. I thought he was just using it to pay informants. But kid informants?

The kids all shook their heads. "Don't have much left, just the blocks near the grocery store and the old warehouse. The *target* hasn't been sighted."

He nodded. "That's about eighty percent of the neighborhood. Remember, you'll get a finder's fee as well."

The children saluted James. "Yes, sir, Mr. Brownstone. We'll find him."

They all turned and scampered off.

James closed the door and grunted.

"What the fuck was that?" Shay gestured to the door. "Please don't tell me you're using kids to look for bounties now. Kids are stupid. They won't know to stay away. They'll get excited and draw attention to themselves."

She winced at a sudden thought.

Lily's not a kid, she's an older teen, and she can see into the fucking future, even before counting her reflexes.

James headed back to the couch and dropped down across from Shay. "Nah, I wouldn't need kids to look for a bounty. I've got them looking for something else." He shrugged and scratched his chin.

Shay narrowed her eyes. The last thing she needed was an evasive James Brownstone.

"Care to elaborate?"

He blinked. "About what?"

"On what exactly they're looking for?" Shay gave him a

wicked grin. "I could get Peyton involved and save you some time."

"It's not a big deal. Just a way to get some help and give the kids extra money." James grunted and shrugged.

Shay laughed. "You're a shitty liar. Even Alison's better at lying than you."

He frowned. "What's *she* lying about?"

She smirked. "Just saying. But we're not talking about her, we're talking about you and what you're keeping from me."

James muttered something under his breath. "Dog."

"Dog?" Shay frowned. "Huh?"

"I told you about that dog I saw the other day. I'm sure it's the same one I almost ran over with my truck."

Shay nodded slowly. "Yes, and..."

James shrugged. "I think it's still in the neighborhood. I don't have time to go all over the neighborhood myself, so I've been paying the neighborhood kids to keep an eye out for it. It's not like I have Alison around to see his soul energy in the distance."

She sighed and shook her head. "Don't you think you're obsessing a little over one stray dog?"

"No." He pursed his lips. "Tyler, maybe?"

"Tyler?" Shay blinked. "Are you saying you're going to call Tyler up and ask him to help you find a stray dog?" She laughed. "Seriously?"

James nodded. "Yeah, good point. That fucker would never let me hear the end of it."

Shay stared at James.

That's not what I was getting at, and why the hell would Tyler even know where the dog is? I should do something about this. I should stop *this. If he's this OCD about the dog now, he's probably not ready for it.*

James nodded, mostly to himself. "I'll figure something out."

Shay just sighed and slumped in her seat.

"What's wrong?" James asked.

"Nothing. Just thinking about dogs. Ever thought about getting a poodle?"

He snorted. "No."

Shay smirked. "Just asking."

Kathy stepped out of her car and took a deep breath. The nearby streetlights flickered. The last thing she wanted was to wander around in pitch-black darkness after a long shift working at the Black Sun.

Geeze. Can't they do something as simple as make sure our street lights are working? Welcome to LA, where the politicians love your taxes, and they love spending them all on hookers and blow.

She slammed her car door and locked it with her key fob before heading toward the stairs leading to her apartment. Her heels clacked on the cold concrete.

Kathy's feet hurt. Tyler insisted she wear heels while she worked at the Black Sun to play up her sexiness. Of course, every little advantage led to extra tips. She was under no illusion that she wasn't attractive. She depended on it.

Only an idiot didn't use every advantage available. She'd always been smart, probably too smart for her own good, but careful cultivation of her sexiness ensured a lot of men would evaluate her with their dicks and not their brains, which meant they underestimated her. Even Tyler.

Still, sometimes playing up that sexiness hurt, especially after a long day on her feet.

At least now I have some chance at a future, rather than when I was stuck as a pet of that mob asshole in New York.

Kathy blew out a breath. She had a new life now in a new city, and she needed to take advantage of all her chances to build up her own business and not be so dependent on Tyler.

She slowed as she closed on the stairs, listening, and her heart sped up. There was nothing but the distant sound of cars and wind, but she couldn't get over the feeling of eyes watching her.

Maybe I just let that freak in the warehouse get into my head. I'm fine. I don't...

Movement in the shadows by the bushes caught her attention.

Damn it. Shit.

Kathy ripped her gun out of her purse and pointed it toward the bushes. "Don't think I won't put every bullet in this gun into you. Turn around and run the fuck away with your hands above your head."

The shadow continued to move, but she couldn't see anyone.

Still hiding under the bushes, asshole?

"Show yourself, or I will blow your head off."

She only didn't fire because she didn't want to risk nailing some poor cat or teen who'd been running around without his parents' permission.

A shadow shuddered and moved, detaching itself from the wall and moving past the bushes until it reached the sidewalk. She blinked, trying to find the source of the shadow, but there was nothing.

"What the fuck?"

The form stalked toward her in the shape of a large man, an insubstantial twitching mass of darkness.

Kathy gasped and stumbled backward, keeping her gun up. "I don't know who or what the fuck you are, but this is your last chance before I open fire."

The shadow man continued to stalk silently forward.

Kathy shattered the still of the night with a single shot at the advancing mass. Surprisingly, the sound was muted, as if something were swallowing it. The shadow vanished when the bullet struck it.

She blinked several times, not wanting to believe what had just happened but unwilling to dismiss it. Magic made all things possible.

Swallowing, she marched toward where she'd seen the strange sight. Something glinted in the dim illumination from the streetlights—the crumpled remains of a bullet.

Shit. I definitely *hit something.*

Kathy took a deep breath and ran toward the stairs. She hurried up them toward her apartment, ignoring her sore feet. Upon arrival at the top, she tapped the code into her lock, and the door clicked open.

She stepped inside, turned on the lights, and slammed her door shut. She slapped the lock button and took several deep breaths.

What the fuck was that all about?

Kathy stared down at her gun and took several additional deep breaths before tossing it back in her purse. That was why she carried the damned thing. Protection. She'd just never expected she'd need protection from a random shadow monster.

She slumped to the floor, her back against the door.

It wasn't her first time ever killing someone. She'd been forced to when she left New York, but it was her first time killing some weird shadow man.

Her phone rang, and she pulled it out of her purse and frowned. Unknown number.

What now?

"Hello?"

"Excellent," replied a hollow and wheezing voice. She recognized it instantly. The Eyes.

Of course. I should have fucking known. The son of a bitch.

Kathy sighed. "I take it the weird shadow man was your doing?"

"Yes. I needed to test you."

She snorted. "Did you test Tyler this way too?"

"No. Every relationship is unique, and every relationship must be tested in its own way." He let out a wheezy laugh. "It was interesting."

At least I don't have to look into his creepy eyes without a body this time.

Kathy blew out a breath. "Okay, so what was the test? To see if I walk around armed?"

"No. Many carry weapons or magic to defend themselves. A weapon proves nothing. No, I needed to test if you are brave enough to live. I value relationships only with creatures who possess such bravery."

"So I passed?"

"Yes." Another quiet snicker followed. "I look forward to getting to know you in the future."

Kathy shuddered. *Geeze, is this thing trying to establish a business relationship or hit on me?*

"Another test is coming soon," the Eyes continued. "Danger is coming. Find it and stop it before it comes. If you can, you might be worth paying more attention to. If not, no bother. Disappointments are common in life and...death."

Kathy frowned. "Danger? To the city?"

"Among other things."

"Don't you care if someone messes up LA? That's got to affect you, too."

The Eyes responded with a wheezing laugh. "This entire city could die, and I wouldn't care. I'd just move on. I only care to test you, little girl. If you're still alive soon, perhaps we'll talk."

The line went dead.

Kathy stared at the phone for several moments before shaking her head. She had a newfound respect for Tyler. If this was the kind of shit he had to deal with on a regular basis, he had far bigger balls than she'd given him credit for.

Fuck it. I might regret it later, but if I'm going to up my information broker game, I've got to start playing with the big boys.

CHAPTER TWELVE

Trey yawned as his eyes flickered open. Zoe's popcorn ceiling was still unfamiliar, but once he realized where he was a comfortable smile took over his face. That was, until he saw the writhing tendrils and sharp teeth on the bright yellow plant looming over him. It looked like an odd mix of a fern and a Venus Fly Trap.

"What the fuck? You are the ugliest-ass plant I have *ever* seen."

The maw dropped toward him, and Trey's hand jerked up to the stem, pushing the whole thing back. He squeezed for a few seconds before realizing it was pointless. It wasn't like he could choke out a plant. The tendrils wrapped around his arm.

"Motherfucking weak-ass photosynthesizing sonofabitch. Fuck you. I'll show you why animals rule this motherfucking planet."

A floral mist spread over him from behind and the plant stopped moving, the mouth closing entirely.

A soft, feminine sigh sounded behind him. "Sorry. I'd forgotten to treat it with the mist before bed last night. A certain man of great sexual endurance distracted me."

Trey let go of the plant and shrugged. "Shit happens."

Zoe sat on the end of the bed, naked and glorious, a soft smile on her face. She crossed her arms beneath her ample chest. "I'm very impressed. Many men wouldn't react instantly and would still be disturbed afterward."

"Ain't no problem. That's not even the strangest thing that's tried to kill me this week." Trey chuckled. "Some of those leftover Council guys were fucked up. I don't know if they were from Oriceran or summoned from Hell or some shit."

Zoe's smile faded. "I forget at times just how dangerous your life is. I suppose I shouldn't, given how many healing potions I'm supplying your agency with these days." She shook her head. "James Brownstone is like a fire. Fire is glorious. It can do so many things, and warm you on cold nights. Humanity would have been nothing without it, but I worry for you and your friends—that you'll be consumed by that fire."

Trey snorted. "I can handle myself around the big man."

She crawled toward him to stare into his eyes, her face right in front of his. "Your friend died, though. Doesn't it disturb you?"

Trey nodded slowly and shrugged. "You have to under-stand, Zoe. We all were nothing but gangbangers before. We all were gonna die doing what we were doing, except over stupid shit like turf and drugs, not defending the planet from weird-ass magic bitches."

"And what of James? Did it affect him at all? Sometimes

I wonder about him. A man who bathes in so much blood —can he truly have a heart?"

Trey laughed. "Damn. You ain't seen him around his daughter." He waved. "And don't be thinking he didn't give a shit about Shorty. He's more busted up than any of us, even if he don't show it on the outside. He gives a fuck, and he shows it all the time in his own way."

Zoe tilted her head, her eyes filling with curiosity. "Oh?"

"Yeah. Not just the healing potions, but the anti-magic deflectors. The big man's pouring a shit-ton of money into protection. I don't see all the books, because most of the accounting is done by an outside firm, so I don't even know how profitable the agency is. I mean, he had piles of cash from years of hunting before, but he's probably barely turning a profit." Trey slapped his hand on his chest. "Because he gives more of a shit about making sure we're okay than making a profit."

Trey hopped out of bed buck naked and started pacing. "Not only that, but he leads from the front. The last Council raid...you should have seen that shit. Brother comes marching right in there and just takes it when these wizards are going all firing squad on his motherfucking ass. I don't care how badass his artifacts are, that takes huge fucking balls." He stopped pacing to stare at Zoe. "I ain't got nothing but mad respect for James Brownstone, and I know the best way to honor Shorty is by continuing to take down pieces of shit with the big man."

Zoe's breath caught, and she blinked several times. "I'm...impressed. I don't know if that's brave or foolish, but I'm impressed."

He grinned and shrugged. "I've got to be me." He glanced at the clock. "Shit, also have to get going soon."

She stuck out her bottom lip in a pout. "Could you spare maybe a few minutes?"

"Why?"

The witch ran her hand over her body and licked her lips. "Because I'd like a little more fun before you leave."

Trey shrugged and hopped on the bed. "I'll just tell them I needed a little exercise. This shit's a better workout than PT with the staff sergeant."

Shay took a bite of her scrambled eggs and set down her fork. She stared at James as he gobbled down bacon as if pigs were about to go extinct. Worry knotted her stomach as she thought about James getting blasted by the wizards.

His amulet can adapt to a lot, but he shouldn't always assume he'll be okay. Just because the Council wizards tended to use a certain type of magic didn't mean another batch would. The damn thing's impressive, but it's not going to save his life if someone rips his head off.

Her heart sped up at the thought of James dying. She almost wanted to laugh. She'd spent so many years not giving a shit about anyone but herself. Even her friends were either covers or people she'd betray with little thought, but now she loved a man enough to have trouble imagining what the future would be like without him.

Damn. Old Shay would kick my ass for being such a little weepy bitch.

"Ever thought about quitting?" she murmured.

James looked up from his plate. "Quitting what? Bacon? Fuck, no." He frowned. "If I had to choose between bacon and barbeque I'd choose barbeque, but otherwise no."

Shay laughed. "It always comes down to meat for you, doesn't it?"

"Yeah. What's life without good meat?"

She licked her lips. "Something I ask myself a lot." She waved a hand and laughed. "We're getting off-track. I'm not talking about bacon."

James grunted. "Then what *are* you talking about?"

Shay shrugged. "It's just something I've been thinking a lot lately. You've always been a badass, but over this last year your reputation has spread in a big way, and you've taken on enemies who were crazy-stronger than you've ever handled before. With my help, you've destroyed two international criminal organizations. You fought off an entire army of hitmen. You took down a psychic monster despite having more baggage than a United flight between Los Angeles and Atlanta. In Japan, even though I helped, you killed five of the top hitmen in the world." She shook her head. "You took down the Queen of the Drow in a one-on-one fight, not to mention being key in taking down the Council, a group so tough that several other class-six bounty hunters died taking them on, along with special forces troops."

A smug grin settled on James' face.

Damn it. I didn't mean to fluff him.

Shay scrubbed a hand over her face. "The point is, you went from a badass to a next-level badass."

The grin faded. "Yeah, I did a lot of that shit, but I also

had help, like you said. Not just you, but Peyton, Heather, and the guys from the agency. Maria. Fuck, even Tyler."

Shay took a deep breath. "The higher you punch, the more people are noticing you, both good and bad. That means cities like Detroit and Vegas, let alone the feds, are throwing big jobs at you, but you've had a lot of assholes target you. That's a big reason you had to take on a lot of those guys. The Drow, the Harriken, and now those last remnants of the Council."

James frowned. "The Drow had nothing to do with me being a bounty hunter. They were trying to get to Alison."

Shay rolled her eyes. "And you got involved in all that because you're a bounty hunter. Look, I'm not saying anything about Alison. I love her too. I'm glad you saved her, and I don't regret helping you take out those Harriken, even if we didn't save her mother. I'm more concerned about how many new enemies you're picking up and what that might mean for your continued ability to keep breathing."

He snorted. "It's been nothing we can't handle, even these Council assholes. We've taken out the safe houses, and we took out all those fuckers in the tunnels. No one got seriously hurt." He shrugged. "Well, no one on our side."

She pursed her lips. "It's just something to think about. You've got a daughter now. It's important to think about *her* future too."

James' face twitched.

Damn, that was a low blow. I shouldn't hide behind Alison like that, but anything to at least get him thinking about this shit.

Shay held up a hand. "I get it. I was a killer for a long time. It was hard switching jobs."

James shook his head. "I'm not gonna stop being a bounty hunter just because a few assholes have tried to kill me. I'm still more annoyed they damaged Phillips than that they tried to kill me. People being after me is nothing new. The Harriken and these Council assholes were a little tougher than what I had to deal with back in the day, but I've gotten tougher, too, and not just because of Whispy Doom." He grunted. "Don't really care. What would I even do if I quit? I like to think I could open a barbeque place, but I'm not a businessman. I'd probably punt some fucker through the wall the first time he talked shit about my sauce, so I'll keep taking down assholes until I need a walker. You really that worried?"

"I don't know." Shay shrugged. "I just worry every time I leave that some fucker's gonna come and kill you, and I won't be there to have your back." She sighed and grinned. "If you *do* die, I'm gonna be forced to go on a bloody whirlwind tour of vengeance, and that's gonna keep me really busy."

James grunted. "I'll try to make sure I only die when you're on vacation."

"That would be helpful."

He chuckled. "Doesn't matter for now. The Council's finished. He Who Hunts is dead, or he would have already shown up. I think it was just a few of their low-level punks trying to prove some shit or going off of final orders." He grinned. "You should be happy. I'm gonna take a few weeks off and concentrate on barbeque. We need to get the PFW team ready for our next competition. It'll be nice and relaxing, good bonding for the guys, just them on a few low-level bounties. They're all taking Shorty's death well, but they've also been very busy. I don't want to run them into the ground."

No problem with encouraging him to focus on his barbeque team for a while.

Shay smiled. "That sounds good. It's not like Los Angeles will fall apart just because you don't kick half a dozen asses a month. Relax and obsess over barbeque for a while. Save the beatdowns for judges who criticize your meat."

He nodded. "Yeah, also gives me more time to find the dog."

Shay winced and shook her head. "I don't know if you're ready for another dog."

"How the hell can I not be ready for a dog? I had a dog for years." James looked and sounded more confused than angry.

She sighed. "Maybe it's more that I'm worried about the city."

"Worried about the city?"

Shay nodded. "If someone hurts your new dog, you might destroy the city." She shrugged. "If you want a new pet maybe you should get one, but that random stray dog isn't your responsibility. Why not go to a breeder or a shelter or something? And the dog might not even be a stray. Maybe it already wandered home to some other barbeque-loving bounty hunter. If you pick one out yourself, you'll be able to make sure that it's perfectly suited for your personality."

"This isn't about me. It's about the dog." James shook

his head. "If he's not a stray, then his owner is a fucking moron. He shouldn't let his dog wander the neighborhood where he might get hit by a car. That's fucking irresponsible. Dogs get out, sure. Leeroy did on occasion too, but I've seen that dog a few times now, so I don't think he's got an owner."

"What are you going to do? I know you have the Little Rascals running around trying to track the dog. Are you going to use your bounty hunter skills to track down a stray dog?" Shay snorted. "It's not like you can go rough up raccoon informants for his whereabouts. He's a *dog*."

He sat there for a moment, his brow furrowed.

Oh, shit. I just gave him an idea, didn't I?

James grinned and nodded. "You're right, Shay. I need to stop thinking of this dog like a stray and start thinking of him like a bounty."

Shay chuckled. "What does that mean? Do I need to tell all the raccoons to get out of Los Angeles County?"

James shook his head. "I got a good look at the dog, good enough that I have those kids running around searching for him. I'm sure Heather can do some of her shit with drones and find him. Algorithms or some shit like that. This isn't about me *getting* the dog. I just want to make sure he's okay. If he's someone's dog, I'll have a conversation with them about proper pet ownership."

"I'm sure that will be painful for them." Shay smirked.

James shrugged. "If they've been a bad owner. If not, then I can take the dog to the shelter until I'm ready for a new dog."

"Chihuahua?"

He stared at her.

She shrugged. "The contrast would be hysterical." She sighed. "You're no fun."

James grunted.

Okay, so James is getting a new dog soon. Oh, I really, really hope this dog isn't a furry little shit.

Shay cleared her throat. "Just curious. Setting aside breed, if you had a dog, what would you name him?"

She worried about him going with Leeroy II.

James frowned. "Don't know. Hadn't thought about it much."

Shay nodded. "Okay. Do what you need to do, but I can't call Peyton back from vacation for this."

"It's okay. Between the kids and Heather, I'm sure we can find the dog." James nodded, his face filled with determination.

If he can take out the Harriken and the Council, he can find one stupid dog in his neighborhood.

CHAPTER THIRTEEN

"James hasn't called Heather yet, but it's only a matter of time," Shay explained and picked up her fork. "This is a new level of obsession."

Maria shrugged. "Sounds like a man who needs a new pet. I'm not much of a pet girl myself, but I can understand the bond between a man and his dog."

She munched on her forkful of salad as Maria sipped a lemonade. As much as Shay liked some of her other friends, they all still believed she was only an archaeology professor. Since Maria knew the truth, it made hanging out with her far more relaxing—such as with today's refreshing lunch date.

Light conversation and equally light jazz flowed around them at the busy bistro. It wasn't the fanciest place she'd been to in a while, but it was perfect for a peaceful afternoon.

This is what a normal life should be. Okay, maybe not normal, but at least real. Actual friends. Actual people I can talk to without having to remember what lies I told them. People who respect me for what I do and aren't planning on shooting me the first chance they get, or who would run away screaming if they knew the truth.

Shay sighed. "I just hope he's not building up that particular dog too much. He might just be misunderstanding the situation with it wandering around. I don't know. I've never really been big on the pet thing myself. All the men in my life seem to love them, though. And it gives James something to do now that the Council crap is finally over. I wasn't so sure, but if He Who Hunts is still alive, I doubt he would have waited so long to make his next move."

Maria nodded. "Yeah, Tyler hasn't heard anything. I know he's got Kathy chatting with an informant, but all he was willing to spill was the informant didn't have anything else useful to say other than the previous tunnel tip. He's acting cagey, but that doesn't mean anything. I'm sleeping with the guy, and I still think he's trying to figure out how to charge me for information about the location of his apartment."

"Got to accept our men as they are." Shay grinned, and the women shared a laugh.

Maria folded her hands in front of her, her face tightening. "I've got something to tell you."

Shay looked up. "Don't tell me you've heard that Council bastard's still around through the cops or something." She groaned. "I thought this shit was finally over. I like it when my biggest worry about James is whether he's going overboard looking for a dog."

The other woman laughed and shook her head.

"Nothing like that. Barely been paying attention to that kind of thing the last few weeks other than what I hear through Tyler." She rubbed the back of her neck. "I'm not a cop anymore."

Shay blinked several times and set her fork down. "What? I thought you were just on a leave of absence."

"I was." Maria shrugged. "And I've turned it into official retirement. I guess hanging out with you all has corrupted me. I can't take all the red tape and political bullshit anymore. It's not a horrible deal. I've already put in twenty years, so I even get a pension."

"You know my story. Sometimes changing jobs is great for sanity." Shay shrugged.

Maria smirked. "Your old job was..." she looked around, "a little more questionable than being a cop."

Shay winked. "It's all a matter of perspective. Any thoughts on what you're going to do now?"

"I'm...bouncing ideas around." Maria waved a hand. "But I don't want to talk about that right now. I wanted to invite you to my going-away party. The rest of the AET guys are throwing it. Hell, Weber's organizing it." She shook her head, disbelief coloring her face.

"What's wrong with that? Is he shitty at planning parties?" Shay furrowed her brow. She was far from an expert on decent parties herself, other than the ones she snuck into to kill people.

"No, nothing like that. It's just I'm honestly surprised. I'm not an idiot. I know I can be a hardass and a bitch. I've always kind of secretly wondered if most of the guys hated me. It wasn't like they were going to say shit to me when I was their boss, but now that I'm leaving they're throwing me a party." Maria sighed and smiled. "I'm not going to get all weepy or crap like that. Don't worry."

Shay reached over the table and patted her hand. "Glad to hear your guys like you." She leaned in to whisper, "One of the reasons I left my old job was that one of my own friends tried to kill me for a contract, so I know a thing or two about that kind of shit."

Maria blinked. "Seriously?"

Shay leaned back and nodded. "Whose body do you think they found in my old place?"

"Huh. That's definitely a colorful way to change careers." Maria sighed. "You think Brownstone would consider coming? I'd like him there for a few different reasons. He's a big part of why I'm doing this, after all."

"I'll ask him, but he'll probably be uncomfortable unless there is barbeque to distract him."

Maria laughed. "I'll make sure Weber has barbeque there."

Maria's head swam as she leaned against the back of her chair. She'd lost track of how many beers she'd drunk. A quick look around the room confirmed that everyone else in the Black Sun that evening was either swaying or red-faced, except for Tyler, Kathy, and Brownstone. Tyler had insisted that if there was going to be a drunken party at his place he needed to be sober.

"A room full of drunken cops," he had whined. "If they get rowdy, who am I going to call? The fire department?"

Brownstone didn't seem much affected even though he'd drunk plenty of beer. Maria wasn't surprised.

Tyler had cleared out the scum for the evening, leaving only cops, bounty hunters, and their families. Besides Weber and the rest of the available off-duty AET, there were dozens of other police officers, including Sergeant Mack, and their spouses. A handful of Brownstone Agency men were there. The rest were out on jobs, but Trey and a half-dozen others had shown up.

Trey, Sergeant Mack, and Brownstone huddled together at a table, eating ribs and brisket and speaking quietly but with a lot of gestures at their barbeque. When Maria had wandered by their table, they had been in deep discussion over some barbeque minutiae related to their team.

A cop, a bounty hunter, and a former criminal turned bounty hunter. Whatever else I can say about Brownstone, the man brings people together through sheer force of will. That's got to be the definition of a great leader.

Loud rock music blasted over the speakers. A few people were dancing, but most people were sitting or standing, talking and sharing stories. Even without the music, the din created by so many people talking made it hard to hear past one's own table.

Tyler walked over to Maria's table and sat down. Kathy had taken point on handling most of the drinks for the night but needed help now and again, especially when some table decided it was time for shots.

"This is it," Tyler declared. "You can't go back now."

"Wasn't planning to go back." Maria grinned. "Weber

told me that you only gave him a ten percent discount. Stingy."

Tyler shrugged. "If you were talking like a half a dozen people, sure, I could take the hit, but you've got half a station in here, and freaking Brownstone keeps drinking like it's impossible for him to even get drunk." He frowned. "Shit, maybe it is."

Maria laughed. "I'm just messing with you."

Weber staggered over with a beer in hand and sat in an open seat. "I don't know what I'm going to do, Maria. Without you yelling at me about coffee in the morning, I think I've lost my purpose in life," he slurred. He glanced at Tyler. "Does she yell at you about coffee, man?"

Tyler shook his head. "Not about coffee. Everything else, though…"

Both men laughed.

Maria rolled her eyes and turned as she sensed someone behind her. Shay.

The other woman smirked at Tyler. "Yeah, Mr. Pay Per View should be careful he's saying." A hint of menace underlay her words.

Tyler muttered something under under his breath as Shay took a seat.

She smiled. "Nice party, even if it feels weird to be around so many cops in a small room."

Tyler chuckled at Shay. "Now *that's* a sentiment I can relate to."

Weber shook his head wildly. "It's not going to be the same." He set his beer down. "Without Maria busting our balls, the AET is going to get soft."

Maria snorted. "You'll be fine. You all know what to do. You don't need me."

Weber sniffled a little.

She groaned. "Come on, don't do this."

The sergeant stood and shuffled off, his arm to his face.

Maria sighed and stood. She picked up her glass and a fork and banged it against the side until everyone stopped talking and looked her way. Kathy killed the music with a few quick commands into her phone.

"I've chatted with a lot of you individually already," Maria announced, "but I figured I should say something. I asked Weber not to have anyone give any speeches because I wanted to give one, and you all know I don't like people outshining me."

Everyone laughed. Weber laughed harder than anyone else.

Maria smiled. "I've been a cop for twenty years. Beat cop the first few years, then Vice, then SWAT, and then AET. I've worked for the LAPD that entire time." She took a deep breath. "The whole world changed on me and most of us all of a sudden right when I was starting out. Being a cop went from just dealing with criminals to worrying about magic." She nodded at Weber and a few of the other AET officers present. "AET wasn't even a thing at first. I mean, who would have even thought we needed to worry about a special division of cops to deal with magical threats?" She snorted. "Yeah, I know we call them enhanced threats, but we all know what we're talking about. We are the anti-hocus-pocus squad. I am...I *was* the leader of the people who would have put the Wicked Witch of the West in her place if she showed up in LA looking for shoes and Dorothy. I might have never railgunned a flying monkey, but I came damned close."

The gathered crowd laughed, and the AET officers laughed loudest.

Maria blinked her eyes a few times, trying to keep any tears at bay. "Every day we worked together to keep people safe whether from the common criminals or the outrageous high-level bastards." She looked down for a moment in silence. "And we all know that every day we get up in the morning and put on that uniform not knowing if we'll make it home to those we care about." She glanced at Tyler before returning her attention to the crowd. "But we all make that choice because we know that the police represent the thin blue line that keeps this city safe."

The cops shouted their agreement.

She lost the war against her feelings, and a few tears leaked out. "Even though I'm retiring, every day from now on when I get up, I'll think about you all first. Think about the sacrifices you're continuing to make." She wiped some tears from her face. "And how you are the best men and women I've ever known. I've never met finer people than my brothers and sisters in the LAPD. God bless you, everyone, and let's keep having a good time the rest of tonight."

The room exploded in applause, and Maria slumped into her chair. At least if she were crying there, it'd be not nearly so obvious.

Tyler was right. This is it. I'm not a cop anymore.

Weber wandered back over to the table as the applause died down. He waited for a good minute, as did Tyler and Shay, as Maria got her tears under control.

Losing all my ball-busting cred here. Everyone's going to know I actually have a heart.

She blew out a breath. "This is harder than I'd thought it would be."

"What are you going to do now, Maria?" Weber asked.

She let out a quiet chuckle. "Really wish people would stop asking me that. For tonight, I'm just going to do the whole eat, drink, and be merry thing."

He shrugged. "You don't seem really merry right now."

Maria gave him a death glare and he winced, even as drunk as he was. Tyler eyed her for a moment with a slight smirk on his face.

You've done a good job of keeping it to yourself, Tyler. Don't worry. You won't have to keep the secret about my plans much longer.

Her glare shifted into a smile. "I'm only not merry because I'm not drunk enough yet." She winked at Tyler. "Barkeep, I need more of your best ale!"

Tyler stood and shook his head. "Drunk cops are the worst. Even when they are hot."

CHAPTER FOURTEEN

He Who Hunts floated through LA hundreds of feet in the air, considering his options. Between the government raids and Brownstone's tunnel raid, his main forces had been depleted. He'd gathered the raw materials to create more servants, but the energy required was becoming increasingly taxing.

The cars and people flowed beneath him, all wasting their short, pointless lives. One good massive explosion would have done much to make the humans of LA understand the true nature of existence, but his long-term plans would have to come before short-term satisfaction.

Giving up on Brownstone wasn't an option, but He Who Hunts also needed to generate a scenario that would ensure the man felt the rage and anguish necessary to draw upon his true power. Without that, the red crystal would be useless, and all the resources and energy He Who Hunts had expended would be wasted in a scheme as pointless as his Council brethren's.

It was clear now that he would have to face Brownstone directly, but if the bounty hunter came with another army, the fight might be over before the crystal could corrupt the man, or even before the opportunity arose to engage its magic.

The window of opportunity had narrowed and the time for caution had passed. His next strike would need to be bold and force Brownstone into a situation where he couldn't win with his normal tactics. Perhaps a situation where frustration would drive him to the extremes of his mind and soul.

He Who Hunts stared down at the city as he continued floating along. A line of cars led to a massive parking lot. Colorful buildings, roller coasters, and thick crowds littered the ground beneath him: Happy Magic Land Amusement Park, according to the sign out front.

It was the perfect stage for corruption.

It was time to gather his remaining forces.

We're ready to show you what's up, big man, Trey thought to himself as he killed his F-350's engine. He didn't give a shit if it was a tight fit with so many men. He loved that truck.

"Let's do this shit." He threw open his door.

Trey, Deshawn, Max, Carl, Lachlan, and Daryl burst out of the F-350. A row of houses lined the street, yards between each. Their target location was about fifty feet away, an unassuming light blue home.

Lachlan frowned and looked down at his stun rifle. "I can't believe this shit. We're going against a level four without the big man for the first time, and we've got to use non-lethals? That's some bullshit right there, you know what I'm saying?"

Trey shrugged. "The bounty notice was clear. They want this guy alive, probably to testify against some of the crime families he used to work for. We ain't even gonna score half the money if we waste his ass, so we bring him alive, or this is just gonna be a waste of our fucking time."

Lachlan snickered. "Yeah, this ain't gonna be fun."

The men grumbled and checked the power cells on their stun rifles. They all had regular pistols if they needed them. Even if they were trying to take the man alive, no one was prepared to sacrifice a team member for money.

Despite the danger of their foe, they were back in their signature suits, although the anti-magic deflectors clashed with the style and the bulletproof vests gave them a bulkier silhouette.

I should ask Zoe if there's a slicker-looking deflector out there.

The target, Alphonse "Quickstep" Cametti, had been just another hitman out East until on one lucky job he stumbled onto an artifact that gave him a useful power for any man, let alone a hitman: teleportation.

Fortunately for Trey and the boys, Quickstep needed line of sight for his power to work, and it was short-ranged. It wouldn't be a matter of the man just blinking away the minute he felt threatened.

As they closed on the door, Trey's heart rate kicked up, and a grin slipped onto his face. A year ago, he'd just been some punk running on the streets. Now he was taking on teleporting hitmen.

He cleared his throat. "We've been doing this shit for a while now, and we've been training hard at Fort Shorty to deal with magic shit. We took on the Council several times, and their weird-ass monsters and motherfucking wizards had a lot more powers than Quickstep. We'll stun his ass and bring him in. This shit's gonna be easier than our last job, I bet you."

Lachlan furrowed his brow. "How we gonna keep him from teleporting away once we stun him? It'll wear off, and he'll just run like a little bitch, won't he?"

Trey pulled out his phone and tapped at it until an image of a silver pendant formed by seven interconnecting rings was on the screen. "He ain't no Oriceran. We take this necklace off, and he can't do shit. He's just another bitch-ass hitman, then. With cuffs on, he ain't doing shit."

Manuel rubbed his hands together. "What about that necklace? We get to keep it?"

"Hell, no. We have to turn that shit over to the 5-0 along with Quickstep." Trey shrugged. "Don't get greedy, motherfuckers. Now, let's do this like we planned. Lachlan and Daryl, you with me in the front. Everyone else, wait in the back. Spread out in case that bitch teleports. Remember, though, we need his bitch ass alive."

He looked up at the house. Thick curtains covered all the windows.

Trey jogged toward the front door. "Let's prove to the big man we've got what it takes to bring in the big bounties."

Lachlan and Daryl rushed after Trey as the other bounty hunters rounded the corner and headed toward the back.

Trey knocked on the door.

Lachlan blinked. "What the fuck? You're knocking?"

Trey shrugged. "Hey, you never know. We've got a badass rep, especially lately with that subway shit and the Council base. Maybe he'll do the smart thing and give the fuck up. Besides, it ain't like he's always wearing that necklace, just when he's on jobs. Why do you think I decided to go after him as our first solo level four?"

They all raised their stun rifles as the door rattled.

The door opened to reveal a muscular man with a shaved head in jeans and a wifebeater. The teleportation necklace hung around his neck. A disinterested expression rested on Quickstep's face despite three men aiming stun rifles at him from less than a yard away.

Aww, damn. Motherfucker.

Quickstep smirked. "You ain't no cops. Who the fuck are you supposed to be?"

"I'm Trey Garfield with the Brownstone Agency. We're here to take you in, Quickstep, for your level-four bounty. I'm not gonna sit here and list all the people you've killed. We'd fucking be here all day." Trey snorted.

The criminal chuckled. "You are some dumb shits. You think just because you have his name that you're as tough as him? *Please,* fuckers."

Trey glared at him. "Nah, bitch. I think we're plenty tough enough by ourselves. Now, you gonna be a good boy, or are you gonna make this shit hard on yourself?"

Quickstep vanished, and a loud pop from behind sent Trey and the others spinning that way.

The bounty disappeared again as soon as they faced him. Another pop had them turning back toward the front door, but this time the man was already sprinting up the stairs past the living room.

Trey fired at the man, but the criminal winked out of existence and the stun bolt slammed into the wall, discharging harmlessly.

Lachlan scoffed. "Told you this shit wasn't gonna be fun. 'It's all gonna be easy and shit.' Give me a fucking break."

Trey pointed toward the street. "You two go over there and spread out. Don't want him teleporting out of the fucking house. I'll corner his ass inside." He rushed inside and up the stairs.

He crested the stairs and fired a few stun bolts down the hallway, hoping for a lucky hit. All he did was waste more energy as he nailed another wall.

"Where you at, Quickstep?" Trey shouted. "You ain't getting away. We've got the place covered from all angles, and we heard about how you're set up nice here. Maybe if you come in, you can give up those fuckers you used to work for. They'll send you to Witness Protection down in Scottsdale, Arizona or some shit. It ain't so bad."

He held his breath, listening for any sound that might reveal the bounty.

Trey crept down the hallway toward an open bedroom door. The whole house was dark, despite it being the middle of the day, which meant Quickstep hadn't opened any of his blinds or curtains.

What? Worried some other motherfucker's gonna teleport in and surprise you, bitch?

The floorboards squeaked as Trey continued toward the bedroom. With Quickstep's line-of-sight limitation, the criminal would have to open a door to get the drop on the bounty hunter. That fueled Trey's confidence as he moved toward the bedroom. This job would be over soon.

His heart sped up as he noticed a mirror at the other end of the bedroom, his reflection visible in it, and more importantly, the hallway behind him reflected in it.

"Motherfucker."

Trey pivoted a half-second before he heard the loud pop. Quickstep appeared, gun in hand and a vicious grin on his face. The criminal pulled the trigger, and Trey hissed as he fell backward, a wave of pain shooting through his chest and ribs. A bulletproof vest might save his life, but that didn't mean he'd escape without pain or injury.

The bounty hunter pulled the trigger as he was falling, but Quickstep teleported away, the bolt passing through empty space and arcing against the wall as the criminal popped into existence beside Trey.

Quickstep kicked the stun rifle out of his hand and aimed his gun. Trey rolled to the side to avoid a bullet to the head and yanked the man's legs out from under him. The criminal's gun fell out of his hand and slid into the hallway.

With a pop, the criminal teleported a few feet in the air, facing the ground. Trey threw a punch, but the man teleported again.

Trey yanked a sonic grenade out of his pocket and threw it toward the doorway. No groans followed the whine of discharge. Instead, he heard a distant pop from the front.

Motherfucker got out. Fuck, I hope the boys are lighting him up.

Trey forced himself to his feet. His ribs hurt like hell, but he wasn't bleeding, and he didn't want to waste a healing potion on bad bruising. He snatched his stun rifle and jogged down the stairs, each footfall jolting his aching ribs.

You ain't getting away, motherfucker. Not today. You ain't so tough, or you wouldn't be running, motherfucker.

Trey hit the bottom of the stairs and rushed out the front, the bright sunlight forcing his eyes to adjust after the time in the darkened townhouse. He snapped up his stun rifle, ready to nail the bastard even if the damned weapon was shit for long-range shots.

He skidded to a stop and blinked, surprised at the sight in front of him. Quickstep lay on the ground, groaning, already handcuffed. Lachlan and Daryl stood over him, big grins on their faces and their stun rifles over their shoulders. Lachlan kept tossing the teleportation necklace up and snatching it out of the air.

Trey shouldered his rifle. "Damn, boys. Good work. I thought that motherfucker was gonna get away. Underestimated the fucker."

Lachlan and Daryl exchanged glances.

"What are you talking about?" Lachlan asked. "You were the one who took his ass out."

Trey winced and clutched his chest. "Bruised a few ribs. Motherfucker shot me." He frowned down at the groaning criminal. "But what you mean I took his ass out? He teleported."

Lachlan chuckled and nodded. "Yeah, when he popped out here, he fell to the ground, all groaning and holding his ears."

Trey grinned. "So I *did* get him with the sonic grenade." He sneered at Quickstep. "That's right, motherfucker. You ain't so tough, and it ain't just James Brownstone you got to be afraid of anymore in LA."

Daryl winced and grabbed his stomach.

Trey frowned. "He nail you, too, man?"

The other man shook his head. "I think something was wrong with my lunch. Fuck, man. I can't wait all the way to the station."

Trey nodded toward the house. "Use his fucking bathroom. Not like he can complain."

Quickstep let out a loud groan, drool coming out of the side of his mouth.

Lachlan snickered. "You better hurry, Daryl, otherwise you'll end up with a new nickname."

Daryl frowned but edged toward the front door. "What new nickname?"

"Fire-ass."

The other man grunted and broke into a sprint.

Trey laughed and shook his head. "Not bad for our first level four, even if Daryl's gonna need new drawers after this." He looked toward the door as Daryl headed inside with a smile on his face.

We're still living the life, Shorty. Wish you could be here, brother, but we're gonna live twice as hard for you.

CHAPTER FIFTEEN

Maria stood before the thick glass door at the front of the Brownstone Agency, her stomach twisted in knots.

What if he says no? It's not like I can go back to the LAPD after retiring and having a big party. What am I supposed to do, take up macramé?

Maria snorted. If she could face down witches and Drow, she could face a little talk with Brownstone. She opened the door, striding with confidence toward the front desk.

Charlyce looked up and offered her a smile. "Lieutenant Hall, nice to see you. Mr. Brownstone is waiting for you in the first conference room to the left down the hall."

Maria shook her head. "Just Maria now."

The other woman blinked. "Excuse me?"

"I'm retired. I'm not a cop anymore. I'm not Lieutenant Hall."

Charlyce smiled. "Oh, I'm sorry, ma'am. Yes, you're right."

Maria waved. "No problem." She headed down the hall.

She'd called Brownstone earlier to say she needed to talk to him and that she would like it if Trey and Royce were there, but she hadn't explained why she needed them. To her surprise, Brownstone agreed right away without even asking for more details.

Does he really trust me that much? I wouldn't trust me so much after the way I treated him, even if I have been helping him out since then.

Maria arrived at the conference room. The door was already open, and the three men were sitting at the table, all on one side. She headed in and sat opposite them.

Brownstone nodded to her. "Hey, Hall. What's this about?"

Trey frowned. "Ain't more Council bitches coming, are there? If there are, we're ready to fuck them up."

Royce didn't say anything, just watched her, his gaze full of calculation.

Maria cleared her throat. "No, no Council." She sighed and shrugged. "I'll just get to the point. You know I'm retired now and I need a new job, so I wanted to sign on with the Brownstone Agency."

Trey laughed. "Motherfucker. I never saw that shit coming."

Brownstone grunted. Royce nodded and rubbed his chin, a vague look of approval on his face.

Maria looked at Trey. "I will bring a lot of experience to your team. You all know that. I've worked with you before."

Trey waved his hands in front of him. "Hey, I ain't bitching. You're a certified badass as far as I'm concerned. It'll be weird, you being an ex-cop and us all being ex-gang members and all. No man in this agency can deny that, but it ain't my call." He nodded at James. "It's the big man's. His name's on the building and shit."

Brownstone didn't say anything. He looked at Royce, a question on his face.

Royce nodded at him. "We've been talking about needing to recruit more people anyway, and we also need to do something about leadership. With someone like her, it'll be easier and more efficient to grow past the gang structure. We can actually start talking about dedicated squads." He shrugged. "Let's be realistic. Trey's the only real leader we have left since we lost Shorty. Max is decent, but he's just missing something."

Maria remained silent, her neck and shoulders tense as she listened to the men discuss her. She didn't give a shit that they were talking about her like she wasn't there, especially since Royce was giving a lot of good reasons why she should be hired.

Shit. I haven't really had to apply for a job in twenty years, and joining the different divisions was almost a shoo-in with the record and recommendations I had.

Brownstone leaned forward, his brow furrowed. "The Brownstone Agency is a bounty hunting organization. We're not cops."

Maria nodded. "I get that."

"Do you? That means we'll do shit you might not always like. We go after bounties, but we're not running around town trying to lock up every criminal we see. It also means that I, and by extension, my guys, don't always play by the rules." Brownstone shrugged. "You don't have a problem with me now, but it used to be you were prepared to lock me up because you thought I was a dangerous menace."

Maria snorted. "Yeah, and since then I've been doing shit like buying anti-magic deflectors from shady underground elf black marketeers." She took a deep breath and slowly let it out. "If I wanted to still be a cop and always play by the rules, I wouldn't have retired. I'm in my forties, still fit and ready to take down bad guys. I get that you do bounties and not all criminals, but every bounty you go after is dangerous scum. I figured this was a good way to still take down bad guys without so much red tape and without worrying about political crap." She sighed. "Besides…"

Trey and Royce watched in silence.

Brownstone frowned. "Besides what?"

"I need to be with a team I trust. If I tried to build a team of my own, that could take years. I ran with you all against the Council. I know that was mostly me working with Shay, but I saw how everyone worked." Maria looked between Trey, Royce, and Brownstone. "I trust the Brownstone team." She shrugged. "And I figure we both can benefit from this."

Brownstone locked eyes with her, his face unreadable as if he were trying to peer into her soul. A good half-minute passed before he opened his mouth and said, "Welcome aboard, Hall." He chuckled and turned to Trey. "You were gonna do some training today anyway, right? Might as well throw her into the deep end."

Trey grinned and nodded. "Yeah. Good time to test her out. I hear you, big man."

Maria frowned. "What the hell are you two talking about?"

Maria laughed as she zipped up her tactical room jumpsuit. "This is the shit I'm talking about. I don't know how much Brownstone spent on this training room, but I would have killed half the city council to have gotten a training environment like this for AET. VR shit isn't good enough."

The bounty hunters who were suiting up all laughed.

Trey shrugged. He wasn't suiting up because he was supposed to concentrate on observing the whole training session. "The big man likes us to be prepared. Between Royce, this place, and Fort Shorty, how do you think we went from a bunch of street hoods to badasses who can take down wizards and freaky monsters and shit?"

She snorted. "Good point." She looked behind her at the nine men wearing red armbands. "I want to get this shit out of the way. Brownstone said he wanted me to lead your red team against the blue team. Do any of you guys have problems working with a woman?"

Isaiah stepped forward and pulled up his red armband. "We worked with Alison all summer, and we've seen Shay kick a fuck-load of ass. We ain't got no problems with chicks as long as they can keep up with us."

Maria shook her head. "Let me put it a different way. Do you have a problem working with *me*, and more importantly, taking orders from me?"

She stared them all down. Despite her respect for the Brownstone Agency men, they were all young and brave but had limited experience, and they were used to working with their ex-gang friends, not cops. Maria had two decades of experience as a cop, years of that leading highly-trained tactical units.

Isaiah shrugged. "Show us what you got, 5-0, and give us no reason to bitch."

Maria smirked. "Okay, then."

The two teams filed into the mist-filled tactical room. Loud peals of thunder roared from hidden speakers, and a bright flash shot overheard.

That's some convincing fake lightning. If we just clone Brownstone and put one of him in each big city, major crime would shrink to zero in this country.

The ramps and blocks that formed the maze were confusing enough in the normal dim lighting, but the simulated storm conditions would make for a difficult fight for both sides.

"I want five minutes to talk to my team," Maria announced. "Leadership is about planning, not just shouting."

Trey shrugged. "Fine by me. How about you, Blue Leader?" He looked at Kevin.

The other man shrugged. "We'll go get set up." He waved his arm and jogged away. The blue team men followed him, disappearing into the fog after a few seconds.

Maria chuckled and cracked her knuckles. "So, first things first, everyone's going to have a partner. Who's the best shot?"

Several men raised their hands.

She snorted. "I don't have time for a big dick contest. Who honestly is the fucking best?" She glared at the men.

Everyone dropped their hands except Carl.

Maria grinned. "Congratulations, you're a sniper."

He frowned. "How am I gonna snipe shit in this fog?"

Maria slapped the side of the rifle and a flashlight lit. "Your partner's going to watch your ass, and someone else is going to paint your targets." She held up the rifle and nodded. "Good penetration through the simulated fog. Who's the fastest runner?"

Daryl raised his hand. This time she didn't even have to yell at them.

Good. They are naturally accepting my authority, which means I can work with them.

Maria nodded. "Okay, we've got the start of a plan, especially given what Trey explained—that we don't have access to grenade simulators this time. Your DI is good at giving you discipline and jobs as general experience, but I think you could all use a lot more direct breach-and-clear training. That'll turn a lot of your future jobs from potential clusterfucks to curb stomps that are over in less than a minute. Today, though, let's just kill ourselves some fucking blue team."

The red team men grinned. "Let's do this shit, Lieutenant."

She shook her head. "I'm retired now. Just call me Maria."

Ten minutes later, blue-team screams cut through the fog as three men charged up the ramp, hoping to get the sniper who'd been picking off their men. Daryl's spotter job had ended a minute ago since even *his* speed couldn't save him from a crossfire.

Maria and two other men waited, their rifle simulators pointed to the side. They were flattened against the walls as the blue team men charged toward Carl's last position. The attackers didn't even have time to notice the woman and men on either side as the red team opened fire.

The blue team men fell to the floor with groans of pain. Every man knew it was better to just take your hit and fall rather than deal with the secondary shocks.

That leaves only two guys, Kevin and Lachlan, but we're down to four ourselves.

"Carl, get up here." Maria lifted her arm and motioned for the men to follow her. "Okay, we're going to use a basic clearance formation. I'll take point."

The red team men exchanged confused looks.

Maria sighed. She had a lot of work to do. "It's simple. We'll form a diamond. I'll be the top, and Carl will be the bottom. Carl will watch our backs, I'll be pointing forward, and the other two will keep decent firing arcs on my left side and right sides. The main point is we have 360-degree visibility and overlapping firing arcs to the front and sides. Make sense? And I'm in the front, so I'll be the first to go down. Not like I'm hiding behind anyone."

The men nodded and moved into position.

"Let's go finish off those blue-team bastards." Maria smirked and stepped forward, keeping her weapon ready.

This training is nice, but still a lot of things I'd prefer to do differently. Next time I'm going to demand grenade simulators.

They advanced down the ramp in formation. Maria was impressed by how well and naturally they held it. Even if some of their direct tactical training was lacking, their familiarity and trust for each other led to natural teamwork. She could work with that.

A shadow popped around a wall and Maria, and the man to her right lit him up before he even finished turning. His partner thought he was going to get a nice flank ambush in, but the man on Maria's left put three quick shots into him, securing the red team victory.

Maria grinned. "Good job. Still sloppy in parts, but I'll whip you guys into shape."

An alert popped up on Heather's first monitor, so she turned to look at her second to check the details. A half-dozen open windows displayed live feeds from the drones she had flying over James' neighborhood in search of his mystery dog.

Probably creeping people out to have so many drones in that part of the neighborhood.

Heather chuckled.

Just do computer shit.

That was what James had told her, like it was trivial to just throw up some drones and find whatever you wanted. She understood where he was coming from. Enough drones with decent cameras could find a person through facial recognition, but researchers hadn't spent nearly as much time training the dog breed recognition algorithms.

Heather clicked into a highlighted window, the one responsible for her alert, and zoomed in with the camera.

"Another cat. Great."

She sighed and shook her head. That was the fourth dark cat she'd encountered. Six other false positives were for dogs, but at least they had dark fur and were roughly the right size, but wrong breed. Another two had been for raccoons.

It could be worse. At least the algorithms aren't tagging every single animal in the neighborhood.

Another alarm popped up, and she looked at the new highlighted window.

"Wait a second."

A dark-furred dog was eating out of a garbage can behind a small Vietnamese pho place.

Heather dropped the drone's altitude but kept it more than a hundred feet from the dog. She didn't want to spook him. She zoomed in with the camera.

Dark fur. Floppy ears. Decent size.

She brought up a few breed pictures for comparison. He looked like their target.

Heather sighed and shook her head. "Sorry about the next part, boy. Hope this is far enough away that it doesn't spook you."

With a flurry of typing, she set the drone to follow the dog.

The dog wandered away from his garbage-can lunch and padded down an alley away from the restaurant, tail down.

Heather sighed. "You should just stop running away from James. He'll make sure you don't have to eat out of garbage cans."

She picked up her phone and dialed her boss.

He answered before the first ring was complete. "You got something?"

"I've got eyes on the target and have a drone following him now. He was eating out of a can near a pho place, and now is heading eastbound away from it. You know where that is?"

"Yeah. It's close to the park." James didn't say anything for several seconds. "I'm heading to my truck now. Just give me updates on the way."

Heather smiled. "James Brownstone, Scourge of Harriken, Council Slayer, and Dog Catcher."

James grunted. "If I can't catch one dog, I have no fucking business calling myself a bounty hunter."

The F-350 pulled into a parking spot at a nearby park. James knew the place well, as he'd held several community barbeque events there.

"You still got eyes on the target?" James rumbled into his phone.

"He's passed the playground, and is now lying underneath a tree. Can't tell if he's asleep, not without getting closer."

James reached into the passenger seat to grab a foil-wrapped paper plate. "Don't get any closer. Don't want to spook him."

He stepped out of the truck, his plate and phone still in hand as he walked toward the playground in the distance. Resisting the urge to walk toward the dog, James took a deep breath.

This is it.

"Okay, gonna hang up now," James whispered. "Keep an eye on him in case he bolts."

"Good luck," Heather replied.

James pocketed his phone and slipped his second hand underneath the plate, keeping a slow but deliberate pace as he approached the floppy-eared dog.

The animal's head shot up as he approached, but the dog didn't bolt. James pulled the foil slowly off the plate, revealing baked chicken. The dog sniffed the air, and the human nodded.

"Yeah, this is for you." James tore off some meat and threw it in front of the dog. "Sorry I couldn't give you barbeque chicken, boy, but you might not be able to handle it. Learned that the hard way with Leeroy."

The dog sniffed the meat and looked up at James before returning his attention to the food. He licked the chicken for a few seconds before gobbling it up and barking once, his tail wagging.

James grinned and tore off another piece. He threw it a few feet in front of the dog. The animal barked and stood before walking over to eat more chicken.

Soon, a line of chicken pieces spaced yards apart led from the playground to the F-350. James set the plate in the back seat with the last remaining piece of chicken and waited, his arms crossed, watching as the dog continued eating the meat and moving toward his vehicle. It was a delicious treat for a dog that had been eating only scraps from garbage cans.

James took slow, deep breaths as the dog walked closer toward him. Fifteen yards. Ten yards. Five yards.

Come on, boy. Just get in the truck, and this will all be over. You want to keep eating garbage or do you want to actually eat decent food?

Four yards. Two yards.

The dog sniffed the air and eyed James. The bounty hunter stepped away from the backseat. A second later, the dog crawled inside the truck.

James closed the door slowly so as to not startle the dog. The animal looked at him but didn't bark or appear concerned.

He hurried to the driver's seat with a shit-eating grin.

Target acquired. Mission fucking accomplished.

A few minutes later, James opened the door to the garage, and the dog rushed through barking and wagging his tail.

He followed the animal, a smile on his face.

Shay leaned against a wall in the living room, her arms crossed and a smirk on her face. "Your chicken trail plan actually worked?"

James shrugged. "It would have been easier if I could have given him barbequed ribs."

The dog ran into the living room and barked a few times. He sniffed around the carpet for a few seconds before walking in circles and sitting down near the couch.

Shay laughed. "So what's the plan? Does he have any tags? Is he chipped?"

James shook his head. "No tags. I felt around for a chip but couldn't find one."

Shay reached into her jacket and pulled out a thin black rod. "I thought this might happen, so I brought this along." She marched over to the dog and moved the rod slowly over him. She shook her head. "No chip. Shelter it is."

James grunted. "Why does he have to go to a shelter?"

She looked up at him with a soft smile. "Is this the part where I say you can keep him?"

"Just saying it took a class-six bounty hunter backed by informants and a hacker with a drone fleet to find the dog." He shrugged. "I think he's earned a nice home."

"Good little escape artist, huh?" Shay knelt to pet the dog, and he thumped his tail against the floor. "You're one lucky pup."

CHAPTER SIXTEEN

A few days later, James stared down at the dog as the animal devoured more chicken and beef. He'd been given plenty of dry dog food as well, but James saw no problem with extra meat. Any pet of his needed to know the glories of meat and the poor guy's ribs were showing. He needed to bulk up; probably had another fifteen or twenty pounds to gain.

James had called and checked around, and no one had reported a missing dog matching the description of his new pet anywhere in the county. He found it hard to believe the animal was feral, given how even-tempered he was and how he'd taken an immediate liking to Shay and James.

He rubbed his chin and walked to a closet to pull out a leash he'd bought the day before. He'd never thrown out any of Leeroy's leashes, but they'd gone up in the fire when his last house was destroyed.

James marched over to the eating canine and knelt. The dog looked up and him and tilted his head.

"We're going for a walk." James reached down to connect the leash to the dog's new collar, expecting resistance. "My backyard isn't big enough to satisfy you, I'm guessing."

The dog barked and wagged his tail.

Still need a name, but I don't think "Chicken Eater" works.

The dog didn't snap, bark, or bite, just waited patiently for James to connect the leash.

James grunted and led the dog to the front door after grabbing a pooper scooper and a bag from the closet.

They stepped out of his house and walked down the sidewalk toward the park. A few neighbors waved at him from the other side of the street, and he nodded back. The dog barked.

"Nice dog, Mr. Brownstone," called a neighbor, Mrs. Garth. "I thought I heard barking from your place. What's his name?"

James frowned. "Still working on that."

The woman laughed. "Don't feel bad. We didn't name our son until he was a month old."

"I think I can figure out a name before then." He nodded to her and continued along with the dog.

James Junior, maybe? Nah, that sounds fucking lame. Shorty? Not sure if the guys would like that. Can't call him Leeroy. He's a new dog, not a replacement.

He wrestled with names, not coming to any decisions by the time he arrived at the park. Only a single person, a gray-suited man on a bench with a briefcase, was in the park. That didn't surprise James given that it was still early in the morning.

James knelt by his panting dog. "Okay, gonna let you off the leash, but don't run off again. I shouldn't need a hacker and army of kids to find a fucking dog."

The dog barked and thumped his tail on the grass.

James snorted and removed the leash, then grabbed a nearby stick and hurled it into the air. The wood flew in a high arc over the bench and the man.

The man's head jerked up, and he frowned.

"Shit, used too much strength," James muttered.

The dog barked happily and charged after the stick. It skidded to a halt right in front of the bench, and he growled at the man. The man frowned and looked down at the dog.

James jogged over to the confrontation.

The man stood, his hand reaching inside his jacket. James narrowed his eyes at the suspicious bulge.

If you fucking shoot my dog, asshole, you're gonna not like how your day ends. Wait a second. The dog hasn't growled at fucking anyone he's run into until now. Not Shay. Not Mack. Not Trey. Not the Andercarr delivery guy the other day.

"Who are you?" James asked.

The man swallowed and looked him up and down. "If your dog attacks me, I'll sue you."

Something about the man's face made James' own twitch. Maybe it was the barely concealed contempt.

James snorted. "Big fucking deal. I've got a lot of money. Who the fuck are you?"

"Who...Wait." The man's eyes widened. "You *can't* be

him. There's no way. He told me this neighborhood was safe, but *you're* here."

"Recognize me, huh? This neighborhood *is* safe *because* I'm here." James offered the man a feral grin. "I'm James Brownstone. You might have seen me on TV a few times and my house is close to here, so I'm asking you again. Who the fuck are you?"

The man swallowed and adjusted his tie, his hand dropping to his side. "I'm just taking a little break on my way to work. Why should I have to tell you anything? You're just some bounty hunter, not the police." He sniffed disdainfully.

James grunted. "This is my neighborhood, and I've promised everyone that I'll keep it safe, so I like to keep an eye on suspicious people. You look and act suspicious as all fuck."

The man sneered. "How am I suspicious? I'm not a tattooed freak with a mangy dog."

"Don't talk shit about my dog, asshole."

The animal barked several times and growled, taking a few steps forward.

"Screw this," the man snarled.

He opened the briefcase and flung it at James, the air filling with strips of shredded paper. James knocked the case down, but the man had already vaulted over the bench and was sprinting away.

"What the fuck?" James growled, confused by the man and his confetti attack.

He was gonna hand this shit off to someone, maybe? Trade briefcases? What?

His dog matched him.

The bounty hunter nodded to his new dog. "Let's go, boy. Time to kick some ass." He rushed after the man, the dog joining him.

Their quarry vaulted a fence. James charged it, but his dog rushed toward an opening farther down.

Resisting the urge to smash right through the fence, James jumped to the top and pulled himself over. He dropped to the ground and looked around for the man.

There was nothing but houses and trees lining the quiet street, a few cars here and there.

"Where the fuck did he go?"

Loud barking sounded from down the street, and James jerked his head in that direction. The man was running toward an SUV, the dog in hot pursuit.

James ran his way. The man threw open the door of the SUV, but the dog leapt on him and sank his teeth into the man's leg.

The suited man let out a howl of pain. "You fucking mutt. I will kill you." Grimacing and trying to shake the dog off, he reached into his jacket.

With a roar of anger, James picked up the pace. The man yanked a gun out and pointed it at the dog, but the bounty hunter closed the distance. He grabbed the man's arm and forced it up just as the gun went off. With a quick yank, he dislocated the man's arm.

The man screamed and dropped his gun. The dog released his death grip and backed up, growling, blood dripping from his mouth like Cujo reincarnated.

"You fucking son of a bitch," the man screamed. "I will fucking kil—"

James slammed a fist into his face, and the man's head

snapped back and he slumped to the ground, his arm hanging at an odd angle and blood pooling underneath his wounded leg.

"You're damned fucking lucky I held back, asshole," James rumbled. "I should have fucking killed you for threatening my dog. If you know who I am, you should ask around about what I do to people who hurt my dog."

The dog padded over to the unconscious man and tugged at a pocket.

Oh, yeah, no point in talking to the fucker since I knocked his ass out, but what's he got on him? Food? The dog's earned it.

James leaned down and reached inside to find a baggie filled with dark green powder. No, not just powder—dust.

He grunted. The drug, derived from Oriceran plants, had become popular in recent years. It wasn't magical directly, but sometimes magic was used in its production. A few kilograms of dust could easily be worth millions of dollars.

James chuckled. "You picked the wrong park for a drug deal, fucker."

He leaned over to scratch his dog's ears. "Good boy. Maybe I should call you 'Dust.'" He chuckled. "Nah, that's just weird."

A few hours later, someone knocked at James' front door. He glanced at his sleeping dog curled up in a doggie bed in front of the TV before rising to answer the door.

Sergeant Mack stood on the other side.

James grunted. "Didn't know you were coming. We didn't have a PFW meeting today."

Mack shook his head. "Not here about that. I was already nearby, so I figured I'd stop by and talk about that dust dealer you and your dog caught."

James nodded and motioned to the couch. "What, is the fucker planning to sue me or some shit? I'd like to see him try."

The cop made his way to the couch. "Nah, he's got a lot more important shit to worry about. Turns out he's a lieutenant of a huge drug lord. Apparently, your boy decided he wants to go solo, so he flew here from New Jersey to set up shop with some guys locally. Besides all the names and connections he has back East, he's got a lot of people he can flip on here. Vice is crapping their pants. This is basically a best-case scenario for them."

James grunted. "What the fuck was he doing in my park?"

Mack laughed. "The idiot didn't do his due diligence. The guy he was supposed to meet, who Vice has already picked up, suggested it. He didn't tell our boy, but this other guy figured that you cleared out all the local scum in this neighborhood so they could do a major deal with less risk." He slapped his knee. "And that fool runs right into you and this dog. What an unlucky guy."

James looked at his sleeping dog. "He sniffed those drugs right out. Maybe he's a police dog." He frowned. "Not that they usually look like that."

Mack shook his head. "I half-wondered, but, nope. No missing police dogs anywhere in California. Maybe the dog used to work for some drug dealer." He frowned. "Maybe he's just got good instincts. You know, for justice."

Shay emerged from the stairs. James hadn't even heard her, but unlike him, she was good at not drawing attention to herself.

She chuckled. "That dog likes me and he never growls at me, so his justice instincts can't be *that* good."

Mack stared at the dog. "Got a name yet?"

James shook his head. "Nope."

"Leaning toward one?" Mack asked.

"Been thinking a lot, but I haven't come up with one."

Mack grinned. "Then what about Justice?"

Shay snorted. "Last thing James needs is a preachy dog."

James shrugged. "I'll think about it."

Justice? Shay's right. I kick ass, but I'm not a cop. I'm not about justice. Probably can't call my dog Ass-kicker or Biter, either.

James grinned. "Could call him 'Sonofabitch.' That's true, after all."

Shay rolled her eyes. "That was so painfully bad that I think they felt it in Oriceran."

He grunted and scratched his cheek. Naming his new dog was proving harder than he thought.

Francis' mother squeezed his hand. "Keep hold of me, sweetie. There are a lot of people at the amusement park today, and I don't want you to get lost."

He smiled up at her. "Yes, Mommy."

People flowed around the pair, families, children, and

teens, all rushing to different buildings or rides, desperate to get in all the enjoyment they could from the Happy Magic Land Amusement Park. A few costumed characters wandered by, waving and bouncing—Captain Duckster and the Rabbiteer.

A man stood near a tree watching the crowd, his face blank and his eyes covered by sunglasses. A faint red glow shone on the edges of the glasses. If the boy hadn't been staring right at him, he might have missed it.

The boy pointed at the man. "Look, Mommy. That man is magic."

His mother sighed and frowned at him. "Shush, now. It's rude to point at people just because they look different, and there are a lot of people who come from Oriceran to visit this park. I don't think they have amusement parks on Oriceran." She looked around and sighed as she spotted a Light Elf eating a snow cone a few feet in the opposite direction and mistaking him for her son's object of interest. "I'm sorry, sir. He's young. He doesn't mean anything by it."

The elf blinked and shrugged. "Uh. Sure. Okay, then. I'm just going to go back to eating my snow cone now."

The boy's mother tugged on his arm. "Let's go, Francis."

Francis looked back toward the man with glowing eyes and sunglasses, but he was gone. A faint red glow surrounded a rock on the ground.

"Oh, he turned into a rock." The rock stopped glowing. "But I think he died."

His mother glared at him. "Don't make me regret bringing you here."

CHAPTER SEVENTEEN

S hay paced back and forth in James' living room. The dog was following her, not barking and wagging his tail. She was supposed to already be at Warehouse Three arming up, but she couldn't bring herself to leave.

This is a bad idea. Something is wrong. I can feel it. It's like I can smell the damned blood in the air but can't find the body. Something's just not sitting right, but what?

She sucked in a breath and rubbed the back of her neck.

James looked up from the article on seasonal spicing he was reading on his phone. "You trying to walk the dog inside?"

She shook her head. "Maybe I shouldn't go on the tomb raid."

He grunted. "Why? You said it was just some Canadian shit. You don't have to fly halfway across the world for this one. Not like you're gonna have to ride some horse in the desert for days."

Shay stopped pacing, and the dog barked and ran

around her legs a few times before retreating to his doggie bed. "I've just got a bad feeling. I've had it for a while. Not saying it's psychic or magical or something, just years of instinct."

James shrugged. "About He Who Hunts? He's dead, or he ran back to Oriceran to go cry about the Council getting their asses handed to them. Even Senator Johnston said they've seen no Council shit, and they've got half the fucking spy shops in the world looking for them. Tyler hasn't mentioned anything about the Council. There are no Council safe houses left, and no Council wizards. We've wiped those fuckers out. If there are any left, they can join the survivors of the Harriken and the Nuevo Gulf Cartel and form some sort of 'We Got Our Asses Kicked' club." He grunted. "I've got instincts too, you know."

"Yeah. Bounty hunter instincts, which aren't the same as killer instincts." Shay sighed.

James shook his head. "But you're not a killer anymore."

"That doesn't matter, and that floating asshole probably isn't the only bad guy in the world who has a beef with you." Shay crossed her arms. "If it's not some random crazy assassin or serial bomber or whatever, it might be you and Tyler coming up with some stupid idea to do another pay-per-view. Maybe that's what's setting me off. Maybe you're hiding something from me."

He chuckled. "I learned my lesson about that. I'm not doing that shit again."

"Because you got ambushed?"

"No, because you're still bitching about it." James shrugged.

Shay sighed.

Why am I so worried? Because I've been thinking about a future with him so much? Damn it. Love is nice, but it's also fucking annoying at times.

James grunted. "You keep forgetting how I didn't die a single time before I met you. I'll be fine. Go on your raid."

Shay shook her finger. "Death isn't like getting a cold. It only takes once, and if you're already dead, it's not like you can use the wish. Plus, you never know when someone will come at you. I blew that bitch Yulia down a well with grenades, and she kept coming back."

"Yeah, but you killed her eventually."

Shay rolled her eyes. "Yeah, *eventually.*"

"Just saying." James shrugged. "Besides, I'm taking it easy. Not doing any bounties for a few weeks, and I found my new dog, and now the only thing I have to worry about is barbeque. Even Father McCartney's happy. I don't have to go in there and admit much other than cussing. Oh, shit. I did feel a little wrath when I dislocated that guy's shoulder." He rubbed his chin. "But I didn't kill anyone this week."

Shay snickered. "True restraint."

James nodded. "Yeah, it fucking was." He shrugged. "Hard to get into too much trouble with barbeque, and we're not even competing for a while."

"Knowing you, some barbeque demon will attack you while I'm gone."

A hungry look appeared on James' face. "A barbeque demon, huh?"

Seriously, James? There's a hobby, and there's an obsession.

Shay slapped a hand to her forehead. "You probably wouldn't be able to eat it." She sighed. "Okay, screw it.

177

You're right. I'm being a crazy bitch. I'm gonna head to Warehouse Three and finish packing." She pointed at him. "But only because you said you're going to do nothing but barbeque."

"And I still have my promise to Alison about not doing any major building raids without backup."

Shay nodded slowly. "Good. I'll make this little Alberta trip quick." She walked over to the dog to pet him before heading to the door. "You should really settle on a name for the dog soon."

"Jessie Rae?"

Shay shook her head and said nothing as she threw open the door.

James grunted. "Okay, maybe not. Mean to call a dog Jessie Rae when he can't even eat a lot of barbeque."

Kathy stared down at the tablet on the bar. She'd been scouring the dark web for days now but couldn't find anything to suggest any unusual risk to the city. Most high-level bounties had been avoiding LA, and the Brownstone Agency had taken down a few level fours who'd dared pop their heads up.

Is the Eyes just yanking my chain? He has to care if something dangerous is coming to LA. He's not immortal, right?

Tyler walked over and looked over her shoulder. "You've been up to some shit lately. Too much. You're distracted. Even *you* have to notice it. Your tips are down."

"The Eyes," she murmured. "He said it was a test. Did

you have to put up with that kind of shit when you first met him?"

Tyler snorted. "When I first met him? You can't do anything with that asshole without him playing games. I'm sure he gets off on it as much as whatever he takes from people who go to his place, and he's never clear at all, but yeah, he gave me a big speech about tests when I first talked to him. Three different things. Fuck, I didn't know what the hell he was supposed to be testing: resourcefulness, ruthlessness, or something else."

Kathy eyed Tyler. "What about bravery?"

"Bravery?" He shrugged. "He tested your bravery?"

Kathy frowned at the tablet. "He sent a shadow man to attack me."

Tyler frowned. "What the fuck? Why didn't you tell me?"

Kathy snorted. "What were you going to do about it? Go to the Eyes and make him apologize? Call the cops? I shot the bastard and that was that, but he called me and told me something was coming, a danger that I needed to find. He made it sound like it would be a big deal, maybe serious danger to the city." She shook her head. "I've been looking around, but I haven't been able to find anything. If anything, things are safer than they've been in a while. Everything's kind of safe by the standards of LA."

Tyler smirked. "Oh, Kathy, I'm disappointed." He smirked. "You're so smart, but still naïve and young."

Kathy whipped her head in his direction. "What the hell are you talking about?"

Tyler shook his head. "He's playing you. It's easy because he's such a freak, to begin with. That's old-school fortune-telling con-artist bullshit. The con artist says something spooky as hell to work the mark, then they'll believe whatever they say right after that."

Kathy frowned. "I don't think he's lying."

"So what?" Tyler shrugged. "He's probably not, but it's a useless warning. This is LA. There's *always* something coming, sweetheart."

Sweetheart? What the fuck?

Sure, Tyler had a good fifteen years or so on her, but there was shit that she just wouldn't stand for.

Kathy's face twitched. "First of all, don't call me sweetheart again or I'll tell Maria about those sites you've been visiting on your computer."

Tyler grimaced. "What sites?"

"You let your guard down too much when you're in the Black Sun, Tyler."

He held up his hands. "Okay, okay, you win."

Her face smoothed out. "Second, it's *my* time to waste, right?"

Tyler shrugged. "Sure. Your time to waste, but I'm telling you, he's just fucking with you." He pointed to a table in the corner. "For now, get them some new beers."

The dog barked as James surveyed the doggie training course he'd set up alongside the main obstacle course at Camp Brownstone. A series of ramps, tires, and cones lay before him.

James nodded, satisfied, and set a plate with a steak at the end of the course.

Doesn't hurt to train the dog a little. Gets him some exercise.

Trey and several of the other men lined the course, curious looks on their faces.

"The Brownstone dog, huh?" Trey rubbed his chin. "We gonna take him on jobs?"

James grunted. "Don't know. Not anytime soon, but might eventually be nice to have a little extra help searching for shit. He found drugs on that guy, after all."

Lachlan snickered. "Your dog ain't gonna do this course for that steak at the end."

The dog barked and wagged his tail happily.

Trey smiled at the dog. "Need to give our furry brother a name."

"Fido," Lachlan called.

Trey snorted and shook his head. "I should beat your ass for that weak-ass name."

James walked toward the start of the course and the dog.

"Cat," Max suggested. "It's all unexpected and shit."

James grunted, and Trey rolled his eyes.

Isaiah slammed a fist into his palm. "Ass-kicker McGruff Brownstone."

The men all laughed.

Trey shook his head, still laughing. "Y'all are terrible at names."

"What about you, then?" Lachlan asked. "What great fucking name you got, Trey?"

The other man shrugged. "I don't have a good name, so I'm keeping my mouth fucking shut."

James arrived at the start of the course. He knelt and

ruffled the dog's ears, then pointed to the steak. "Just follow me, boy, and you can have that nice juicy steak."

The dog barked.

James stood and jogged up the first ramp, and the dog shot after him. They proceeded over another ramp and a few tires before zigzagging through a series of cones and finishing up with a vault over low bars near the end of the course.

The dog rushed over to the steak and started licking it after barking a few times.

The men cheered.

"*That's* how you do shit," Isaiah shouted.

Trey grinned. "Your dog is damned smart, big man."

"Smarter than Lachlan," Max offered.

Lachlan frowned. "Fuck you."

James chuckled and knelt to pet the dog while the animal worked on the steak. "Still needs a name, but now that I've started getting some food in him, I should take him to the vet soon. Probably needs shots and shit. Also a microchip. Maybe I'll take him tomorrow."

The dog lifted his head to bark and wag his tail.

Max shrugged. "I've got a name. How about Lachlan 2.0?"

Lachlan flipped him off.

Shay stared into the mirror of her Alberta hotel room. She sighed and shook her head.

Lily bounced on her bed a few times. "Problem?"

"I wish I had precognition like you."

Lily snorted. "Yeah, it's limited and totally unreliable. Other than that, it's great. Love it."

The senior tomb raider sauntered over to the other bed and sat with a deep frown. "Every instinct in me is telling me something is wrong, and that James might still be in trouble."

"You sure this just isn't you being overprotective?" Lily shrugged. "Not going to tell you your business, but it seems like you're getting more and more protective of James. He's your boyfriend, not your kid."

Shay sighed. "Maybe. Not gonna lie, I'm still not used to the nice feelings and giving a shit. I still don't always know how to react."

Lily laughed. "And I thought *I* had issues with learning to trust." She brushed a few strands of hair out of her gray eyes. "Why are you so convinced he'll be in trouble? Because of that last raid?"

Shay ran her tongue inside her cheek. "Everything just felt...too easy."

The teen stared at her, her mouth open. "Easy? Four wizards ambush James out of nowhere and hurt him, then you guys go have a fight with a bunch of weird-ass crazy monsters in the subway, and that's easy? If those guys had shown up when I still lived in the tunnels, we'd have all been killed."

Shay shrugged. "That's just what it means to hang out around James. We've taken down a lot of fucking deadly enemies together. Maybe that's the problem." She narrowed her eyes. "Something just doesn't feel *complete* about all this—not until I see a few more bodies. Those guys smelled too much like cannon fodder."

Fuck. I hope I'm not freaking Lily out with this.

Lily sighed. "I might have powers, but you have years of experience. If something's not sitting well with you, maybe you should trust yourself, you know?" She took a deep breath. "Everything about the job is easy, or as easy as a tomb raid gets. I'm thinking it doesn't take two tomb raiders to go into a mine with a few traps and grab an enchanted pickaxe."

Shay frowned and shook her head. "I don't like the idea of leaving you just because I'm paranoid."

"Why not?" Lily smiled. "You already told me that I'm ready to solo. This is as good a tomb raid as any to try it. I'm in Canada, not an exotic country. I speak the language, or at least one of the languages, and getting the artifact through Customs will be easy because it just looks like a regular old item."

Shay stood and nodded. "You sure about this, Lily?"

"Yeah, I'm sure. I'm ready." She smiled. "*You* made me ready, Shay. I'm a tomb raider now. Go check on James. The worst thing that happens is you have extra time to go on a date."

Shay grinned. "I need to buy a new plane ticket."

CHAPTER EIGHTEEN

K athy knelt on her couch, her laptop on the table in front of her, and stifled a yawn.

What the fuck time is it? Five? Six?

She looked at the clock.

Fuck, it's already 8:00 AM? I've been at this for hours. Maybe I should have taken that little nap last night like I was thinking.

Kathy blinked her tired eyes a few times and continued scrolling through posts and checking her messages. There was an answer to find. There had to be. The Eyes couldn't have sent her on a wild goose chase. Something awful was coming, and she needed to find, anticipate, and prevent it to prove herself to him. To prove something to herself.

I'm better than anyone thinks.

Tyler didn't understand. He didn't give a shit about anything but money. Being an information broker was just a way of gaining money, influence, and status for him.

A puzzle lay before her now, and Kathy refused to let it defeat her. She picked up her coffee cup and downed some of the now-lukewarm brew. So what if she hadn't gotten any sleep? The damned answer was still out there, hiding from her and taunting her.

Her eyes scanned post after post as she looked for something—anything—that would give her a hint about what might be coming to Los Angeles.

Maybe I need to hit up more informants. There's got to be something more than a bunch of low-level bounties coming to town, but that's all I can find.

With a sigh, she closed the laptop and picked up her phone from the table. She rested it against her head, trying to figure out who she might possibly call. She needed someone who would not only know what they were doing but also had useful information.

Kathy smirked. Tyler wasn't the only one who had cultivated contacts.

Two hours later, Kathy lay on her back with a throbbing headache. She'd called a dozen contacts, and no one had anything more useful than information about the same low-level bounties she already knew about. It was like the entire underworld was saying everything was hunky-dory in greater Los Angeles.

Sure, gangs and organized crimes groups dealt drugs, murdered each other, and spread corruption, but that was all the normal nonsense everyone expected from a town that had been steeped in darkness long before magic had returned to the Earth. There weren't even any rumors about any major gang wars coming. It was like after

Brownstone finished off the last of the Council, all the bad guys in LA decided to keep things lowkey for a while.

The Eyes is fucking with me. Trying to destroy me. If he can see into my head, he might know how I can't leave a mystery alone. Well, fuck him. I'll show him. I'll find something that even he doesn't fucking know about.

Kathy sighed. Time for another longshot—some new players in town led by a teen named Harry. He and his little gang used to be tunnel rats, but they'd come into money in recent months. Rumor had it that one of them had hooked up with a tomb raider, and that was why they'd left the tunnels. Kathy even heard a few descriptions that made her think the tomb raider might be Shay.

Why does everything in this city always come back to Brownstone or someone he knows? It's like he's the damned heart of Los Angeles.

Kathy sighed and dialed Harry's number. The phone rang several times.

"Hello?" he answered finally.

"This is Kathy. I wanted to know if you or any of your friends have heard anything interesting lately."

Harry chuckled. "Interesting? We hear a lot of interesting things. Can you narrow it down?"

"Magically interesting. I don't care about anything else. You know what? Less interesting—maybe a weird rumor that everyone else is ignoring, but you and your little gang happened to pick up on."

Kathy didn't care that desperation had crept into her voice. She hadn't slept, and she hadn't eaten anything since the night before. Right now, only one thing would satisfy her: an answer.

Harry coughed a little. "Okay, I do have something. Nobody's asked about it, so we haven't volunteered it. It's not that important from what I can tell, so I'll let you have it for…a quarter of what I charged you last time. I'm telling you, though, it's probably not worth it."

"But you're still planning to charge me?"

"Do you give away information for free?"

Kathy snorted and threw open her computer, bringing up one of her crypto wallets. "Aren't you the industrious one?" She entered the transfer information and hit Send. "I've done it."

"One sec."

The silence stretched for several long moments.

Harry laughed. "Okay, thanks for the money. One of my friends was at Happy Magic Land Amusement Park the other day."

"Amusement park?" Kathy snickered. "Doing what? Trying to get a princess' autograph?"

"The reason isn't important," Harry replied flatly. "The thing is, while she was there she saw something weird. A couple of times. People with weird, flat expressions, sunglasses, and maybe glowing eyes, but she kept losing track of 'em."

"That's the big piece of information I just paid you for?"

Harry chuckled. "I told you it probably wasn't worth it. Just saying they were acting strange, and when one of us notices strange things, it should be hard to lose us while we're watching. Maybe it's some Oricerans just running around with a spell to make them look human, but that's all I got. The tunnels have been clear since Brownstone did his thing. All quiet out there. Quiet for LA anyway."

Kathy scrubbed a hand over her face. "Okay, thanks. Enjoy your money."

"I will."

She ended the call and tossed the phone on the couch beside her.

Kathy groaned and rested her face in her hands. That was the best she could come up with—weirdos at an amusement park? Tens of thousands of people visited the place each day. Just based on statistical probability, she expected a few strange people to show up, whether from Earth or Oriceran. Harry's information proved nothing.

She let out a long sigh and picked up her phone again. Maybe she'd failed the test, but this was the only lead she had. She pulled up the call history and dialed the number the Eyes had used when he'd called her after the shadow ambush.

"Khalid's Falafel Kingdom," answered a loud, cheerful voice. "We've got the best falafels in all of LA. Your mom will cry with how good they are."

"Falafels?" Kathy blinked. "I'm looking for the Eyes."

"Huh? Look in the mirror. You'll find some eyes there. Now do you want to place a falafel order or not?"

Kathy groaned. "Sorry. Wrong number."

She hung up and rubbed the bridge of her nose. Tyler had mentioned to her that the Eyes liked to constantly change phone numbers. He wasn't sure if it was a security measure or a way of making people come to him, but that meant she only had one choice if she wanted to follow up on her stupid amusement park clue.

She sniffed her sweat-soaked pajamas. "I need a shower first in case that asshole can actually smell."

An elf and a human guard in front of the Eyes' room opened the doors. Given the way the human was leering at her, she would have preferred the gnomes.

Kathy stepped into the smoke-filled room, her head throbbing. The painkillers hadn't done much, and she suspected she'd suffer until she caught up on her sleep.

Guess I'm not going to the Black Sun tonight.

"Kathy. Brave little Kathy," came the voice of the Eyes, seemingly from all around her.

She turned slowly, looking for those familiar yet unsettling yellow eyes, but she couldn't find them.

"Be quick, girl. I've business I wish to attend to."

Not like I want to be here, asshole.

Kathy took a deep breath. If she asked him a question, he'd just fuck with her. The only choice was to feign confidence.

She plastered an arrogant smile on her face. "Something's going to happen at Happy Magic Land Amusement Park."

A wheezing laugh sounded beside her. Kathy turned that way, but she still didn't see him.

"Clever girl, indeed."

Kathy shrugged. "I can find out things. What's going to happen there?"

"Why should I tell you?"

She didn't bother to hide her scowl. "Because it's part of your damned test. The fucking danger you said is coming."

He let out another wheezing laugh. "Oh, you have no idea how delicious all this is proving."

Is he getting something out of fucking with me, or is he just enjoying it?

Kathy turned. "If that's it, then I've got to sleep. I mean, I've got shit to do."

"Mystery, Kathy," the Eyes whispered. "The same lust for mystery sent you to a man you shouldn't have been with in New York."

She snorted. "If that's supposed to impress me, give it up. Just because I keep a low profile doesn't mean I think no one knows what I've done before or where I came from."

A frigid touch brushed her neck, so cold it burned. Kathy hissed and spun around. This time, the yellow eyes were there.

"You want to know about the park?" the Eyes wheezed. "I'll tell you, but there'll be a cost."

Kathy kept her face calm. "A cost? What cost?"

"You'll owe me."

"Owe you what?"

He backed up. "The answer to one mystery in the future."

What the hell does that even mean? You know what, I'm too damned tired to care.

Kathy shrugged. "Deal."

The Eyes chuckled. "Fine. To know the future is to alter the future. I'll give you the information you want, but you'll have to make a choice right now. Once I tell you you'll fear for others, and I can see into you. I know you care too much about the lives of others."

She rolled her eyes. "I admit it, I'm not a heartless bitch."

"If I give you the information you need, you can't go to the authorities. You will tell no authorities or those who will tell the authorities." He let out a dark chuckle and wheezed. "If you do, I'll kill you, and I'll make you suffer greatly before you die."

Kathy swallowed. "What's to stop me from walking away right now?"

"If you do, others will suffer and die, and not by my hand." The Eyes vanished and reappeared in a corner. "Not that it matters. Even if I didn't dangle the lives of innocents, you'd want to know. You can't stand it—not knowing. It's a weakness and a strength."

Kathy fisted her hands, prepared to leave. She turned, ready to throw open the door, but she couldn't make her feet move. "Fine. I agree to your terms."

"Good," he rasped from behind her. "It's simple. At noon at the amusement park death will come. Children will weep, victims of the Council's last gasp of relevance."

Her eyes widened, and she glanced down at her watch. "Noon? That's a little over an hour from now."

"Yes, and remember our deal. Solve the problem without the authorities or forfeit your life."

Kathy sat in her car, her head against the steering wheel, not sure what to do. The Council obviously was going to attack Happy Magic Land Amusement Park, but if she called the police and they sent AET she died. She thought about going to the park and trying to warn them, but they might immediately call the police.

She had no idea about the exact nature of the attack, so it wasn't like she could warn them off with a generic bomb threat or something. Even that would bring the police, and without more information, going there herself would be pointless.

I'm in over my head. Maybe Tyler will have an idea.

Kathy lifted her head and grabbed her phone, ready to dial her boss before frowning.

No, he's dating an ex-cop. He'll tell her right away, and she'll demand the cops get involved.

"Shit, shit, shit." Kathy groaned and slumped in her seat. Her hair was a mess, and she had bags under her eyes the size of a Kilomea. "Damn, I'm a mess. Surprised that guy was even bothering to check me out."

There had to be someone who could take on the Council, wouldn't ask for immediate payment from her, and wouldn't feel the need to go to the cops right away.

Her eyes widened, and she picked up her phone. She brought up her contacts list and dialed, her heart pounding.

This has to work.

"Yeah?" rumbled Brownstone on the other end.

Kathy took a deep breath. She needed to project confidence, not desperation. "Brownstone, I have a little free tip I wanted to offer you."

"Free?" He grunted. "Why free?"

Kathy let out a little chuckle. "Maybe I figure being on your good side would be useful."

"It hurts less. What's your tip?"

She sighed. "Okay, I'll tell you, but there are a few other things I need to tell you first…"

CHAPTER NINETEEN

Trey frowned as he picked up his chest armor.

Should have known this Council shit wasn't over. Fuckers going after an amusement park? They ain't nothing but a bunch of weak-ass terrorist bitches. I can't wait to put a few bullets in their faces.

Trey strapped on his armor and put on his anti-magic deflector over it. The other men were gearing up as well, loading weapons or putting on armor. After grabbing a few grenades from a container near the wall, he glared at Isaiah in the corner.

"Get your motherfucking gear on, bitch," Trey growled. "We're rolling soon, and we don't have time to wait on your fat ass. Big man said war footing, so that means hurry the fuck up."

The other man blinked and rushed to his locker.

Maria slapped a magazine into her rifle before adjusting the strap and shouldering it. She marched over to

Trey, maneuvering through the crowd of men rushing around her and gathering equipment.

She frowned at Trey. "We should be calling in AET. This is a clear and present danger to the public, based off what you said earlier."

Trey looked up with a frown. "The big man gave explicit motherfucking orders. The big man almost *never* gives explicit motherfucking orders like that. No 5-fucking-0."

Maria crossed her arms. "Why? Brownstone can't be that desperate for more bounty money from the feds."

Trey shrugged. "Don't know. Don't care. This ain't just a bounty hunting agency, it's the fucking Brownstone Agency. His damned name is on it."

"But we can't just—"

Trey slammed a fist into a nearby locker, the sound echoing. Everyone stopped and stared at them.

He slapped a palm against his chest armor. "We ain't cops, Maria. We also ain't military. We ain't gangbangers, either. We are bounty hunters who work for James Brownstone. That sometimes means that to get the job done, we need to play shit fast and loose. If you can't handle how we roll—" he nodded toward the door, "no one's stopping you from leaving. We all know you're a badass bitch and we respect that, but I want to make it motherfucking clear that first and foremost we respect the big man, and we obey him. You know what I'm saying?"

Maria's face twitched and reddened. She took a few deep breaths. "This isn't about laws or shit like that. This is about innocent people getting hurt."

Trey snorted. "You think the big man don't give a shit

about that? If he's telling us not to call the police, he's got a good reason. He'll handle this shit. We just need to saddle the fuck up and come with the backup he needs."

They locked eyes, both squaring their shoulders.

I like you, Maria. Don't make me have to do something stupid. We don't have time for this shit. James is counting on us.

Maria gave a curt nod and turned to the watching men. "You heard the man. Stop staring at my ass and get the rest of your gear together. We need to get to that park and back Brownstone up ASAP."

Trey grinned. "Glad to have you aboard, Maria." He made a circle with his hand. "The rest of you bitches, we're rolling in five minutes. Don't have time for motherfucking lollygagging."

Isaiah stared at him. "'Lollygagging?'" He snorted. "What are you, two hundred years old?"

Trey glared at him. "Finish getting your gear on, motherfucker."

Shay had just pulled out of her garage in her Fiat on her way to James' house when her phone rang.

"Hey," she answered.

"So, um, how's Alberta?" James asked. "Very Canadian, eh?"

She rolled her eyes. "Yeah, it's very Canadian, but I'm not there. I'm back in LA."

"Already?"

Shay sighed. "I decided to come home. Lily's doing the raid solo." She changed lanes and accelerated. At least traffic wasn't so bad today, which in LA was practically a miracle in and of itself.

"Come home? Why?" Suspicion colored James' voice.

Saw right through me, huh?

"I…had my reasons," Shay replied.

James grunted. "I just wanted to call you to let you know there's a little problem, but you don't have to worry. I've got it under control."

Shay groaned. "Motherfucking son of a bitch. I knew it. I fucking *knew* it. Who just tried to kill you? Did you get them? Did you leave one alive so we can at least interrogate him?"

I don't know if it's my killer's intuition or my woman's intuition.

"No one has tried to kill me," James explained. "I'm going to kill someone at Happy Magic Land Amusement Park."

"Wait for me. I'll meet you there." Shay could hear the dog barking over the phone. "Are you seriously taking your dog to a fight?"

James sighed. "I was taking him to the vet, but I found out I had to go to the amusement park."

"Just fucking wait for me, damn it."

"Nope. It's the Council. We didn't finish them, and they're gonna attack at noon." James let out a low growl. "Fucking cowards."

Shay sucked in a deep breath and slowly let it out. "I know it sounds weird coming from me of all people, but you really need to call the cops in."

"Can't. If I call the cops the person who told me is dead, and maybe others. Can't fuck her over like that."

Her? Not Tyler, then. Maria, maybe?

Shay groaned. "Please at least tell me you're not going there to take on the Council all by yourself."

She made a hard turn, cutting someone off. They honked at her, but she ignored them and accelerated. The amusement park. It'd be damned hard for her to get there by noon; she'd have to speed half the way.

Hope the cops leave me the fuck alone.

"Nope," James rumbled. "Trey, the boys, and Maria are on their way. Just no cops. Don't worry, we've got this shit."

Shay barked a laugh. "And you're going to fight the Council around thousands of people? That sounds like a fucking moronic idea."

James muttered something under his breath. "I'll clear them out."

"How?"

He grunted. "You all keep telling me I'm a celebrity. I'll figure something out with that." Another bark sounded in the background. "It's okay, boy." His voice sounded distant as he said it before growing louder with his next statement. "I'm sorry it worked out this way, but shit happens. See you soon. Won't guarantee I won't kill everybody before you show up."

Shay sighed. "Don't die before I get there."

"Sure. That won't be a problem." James ended the call.

Shay resisted the urge to pound her phone on the dashboard. Sometimes she wondered if the universe was just fucking with them.

James sighed as he waited for the response on the other end of the phone. After Shay's surprise return he'd made a call to Heather, and he knew she'd be confused by what he needed from her.

She blew out a breath. "So let me get this straight. You want me to make sure that no one can call out of the amusement park, and that's despite the fact you're running straight toward the Council?"

"Yeah. I don't want the cops there until I've finished off the Council. I'll make them evacuate the park, though."

Heather sighed. "James, this sounds very, very dangerous."

"I know, but I'm not about to fuck over the person who told me. If it weren't for her, I wouldn't know this shit was going down, and we'd have had no chance of saving anyone."

"Fine." Heather muttered something under her breath. "I'll stop anyone from calling out."

"Thanks. I've got my guys coming, too. Don't worry, I've got this shit."

Heather snorted. "I'm sure that's carved on the tombstones of a lot of men." She ended the call.

Find strong enemies, the amulet whispered in James' mind. *Find strong enemies, kill them, and adapt. Grow stronger. Achieve primary directive.*

Yeah, yeah. Just let me fucking concentrate. Now I get why I should never wear you when I'm driving.

James narrowed his eyes as he changed lanes. This whole day was turning into complete and utter bullshit. He was supposed to be going to the vet, not dealing with crazy magical-asshole terrorist attacks. About the only upside he could see was that if Kathy wasn't blowing smoke up his ass, it was the Council and he could still score supplemental bounties from the feds.

If they can do this sort of shit, that means He Who Hunts is probably still around. If that fucker isn't there this time, I'll pay every fucking informant on this planet until they point me at him and I can fucking finish him off. The Council's pissing me off more than the Harriken.

Yes, Whispy Doom hissed. *Increase power for advanced mode.*

Shut the fuck up.

The amulet continued to murmur in his head, delighted over the imminent violence and death.

The dog barked happily in the back seat. He was in a better mood since they'd changed direction. James wondered if the dog somehow sensed he wouldn't have to go to the vet now.

"We're going to a war zone, boy. This isn't a good thing, and you're still gonna have to get those shots."

James was close now, just a couple more minutes until he arrived at the amusement park. If he had known he was going to take on the Council, he would have armed up better, but at least he had the amulet and all his men coming. Hell, even Shay.

Guess she was right.

He snorted. The only thing he still couldn't understand was why the Council, He Who Hunts, or whoever was responsible for all the recent incidents was so obsessed with targeting him and LA. It made no sense, given how much pain he and his men already had inflicted on them.

Maybe this shit is just revenge. They should have waited

until I was in some cave in Mexico or some shit instead of fucking up a barbeque place, killing innocent people in my city, and now even fucking up my errands with my dog.

James let out a little growl, and the amulet grew more excited.

His F-350 roared into the vast parking lot of the amusement park. He didn't bother to look for a spot, instead zooming straight toward the entrance with the help of jerking wheel movements. Several angry motorists honked at him, and the dog barked a few times, his tail thumping against the back seat.

"This shit isn't a ride, boy."

James slammed on the brakes, the truck screeching to a halt near the entrance. A mass of confused families stared at him like he was a lunatic, several pointing and frowning, some taking pictures.

He threw open the door and jumped out. He'd taken a few steps when he grimaced. It might have been fall, but the southern California sun was still doing its best to keep things warm. He didn't want to leave his rescue dog in the truck on a warm day.

James opened the back door and grabbed the dog's leash. The dog leapt out with a bark, and the pair rushed forward.

Every time someone turned to complain, their eyes widened, and they stepped aside.

"It's James Brownstone," one man shouted.

A woman pointed. "Woah, wait. It's *him*, the Scourge of Harriken."

"Is he hunting a bounty here?" a teen asked. "Oh, man. I'm gonna get to see him kick some guy's ass in person."

James ran past the ticket counter toward the turnstile leading into the park.

The confused attendant blinked a few times at him. "Um, sir, I'm going to have to see your ticket. Even if you are, well, *you*, Mr. Brownstone."

James grunted. "Get me a motherfucking manager right away. We need to evacuate this park."

CHAPTER TWENTY

Another F-350 and two Expeditions rolled up to the front of the amusement park, each filled with heavily-armed bounty hunters.

Trey was the first out and frowned as streams of people rushed from the park, some crying, but no one screaming. He looked up. No smoke. No distant sounds of gunfire or explosions. That was a good sign, and they still had a few minutes until the deadline.

The other men and Maria disembarked, and Trey gestured toward the park and the sea of fleeing visitors.

"Let's go find the big man." Trey rushed forward.

The fleeing crowds parted for the advancing mass of bounty hunters.

"Thank God, it's the police," shouted a man.

"No, no, I think that's the military," another man called.

"We're the motherfucking Brownstone Agency," Trey yelled.

The men forced their way past the fleeing crowds and

through the turnstiles until they arrived at a red brick plaza. A massive castle tower stood in the distance, and various paths of different-colored brick ran off from the main plaza. Electronic signs talking about everything from camera rules to events in other parts of the park filled the plaza, along with discarded wrappers, toys, and bags. The people fleeing weren't doing their best to keep the park clean.

James stood in the center of the plaza with a frown, his head moving back and forth, searching for enemies. His dog was on a leash that had been tied off around a nearby signpost. He barked and ran back and forth, his tail wagging in excitement.

Trey blinked at the sight of the dog.

James turned and jogged toward his men. "Deadline's almost up, but most of the park is already cleared. There might be holdouts, so make sure you don't fucking shoot anything that moves; only the Council or weird-ass monsters." James frowned and looked at his men. "This everybody in LA.?"

Trey shook his head. "Too short a notice, big man. Got other guys coming, but some of them are trapped way the fuck out there. You know LA traffic. Could go smooth, could be molasses. We've got fourteen guys total, not counting you and Maria."

James grunted. "We need to get a VTOL plane or a helicopter or some shit." He nodded to Maria. "It'll have to be enough. This is a simple job. Search and fucking destroy. You won't be able to use your phones because I've got Heather blocking communications. I've got my fucking reasons if Trey didn't already tell you, and I don't want to go into the—"

The entire area shook, and massive spires of scarlet energy shot up from different points in the park twitching and shaking, pairs reaching for each other. Swirling, scintillating portals appeared in the sky over the park, eight in total. The portals descended until the bounty hunters couldn't see them in the distance.

"What the fuck?" Trey shouted.

The other men murmured excitedly.

James narrowed his eyes. "They don't look like the kind of portals the Council was using before. Anything might come out of those."

Maria shook her head and pointed as a father ran past, his toddler in his arms and his wife right behind him. "There are still way too many civilians in this place." She pointed to the portals in turn. "Eight of the damned things, but they're not all in one place. We should split into four teams and sweep the park. There's got to be some way to knock out the portals, and we know some monsters or shit are about to come out." She pointed to a huge map nearby. "Animal Town, Fantasyville, Robotown, and Princess Island. Four zones. Four teams."

Trey glanced at James. He made the call in the end, but Maria's plan sounded pretty damned good to him.

James grunted. "I'm my own team. I'll take Animal Town." He turned and started to jog away. "The rest of you do what you need to, but if you get outclassed, fucking retreat and find another team to back you up. Watch each other's backs."

Trey watched his boss run off before shaking his head

to clear it. "I'll lead a team, Maria another, and Max the last team. Let's do this shit, boys." He pulled his rifle off his shoulder. "Time to save some childhood dreams, mother-fuckers."

James charged along the colorful balloon-lined yellow-brick path leading into animal town. The plaza gave way to huge statues of animals both anthropomorphized and regular, along with more fleeing families and employees, none paying him the smallest attention. Several screams sounded in the distance, and he ran toward them.

Fucking Council. Fucking He Who Hunts. What, you threw a few guys at me, and then fucking chicken out after that shit and pull this crap?

Employees in animal mascot costumes rushed down the path, fleeing from a pair of what looked like alligator men. If it were a movie, the entire situation would have looked ridiculous.

At least the Council is keeping this theme shit appropriate.

James whipped up his .45 and put two rounds into each alligator man, hoping he wouldn't need any anti-magic bullets. The monsters jerked and fell to the ground. He grunted, satisfied with the kills.

There was a loud and distracting hum. One of the portals, most likely.

He jogged further into Animal Town and growled. A pack of eyeless, mouthless, and naked pale-skinned humanoids with long spindly arms tipped with sharp claws rushed around the central square of Animal Town, splashing through the central fountain to throw themselves at costumed employees.

The sound of tearing fabric filled the air, and if he didn't know better, the sound of scraping metal. None of the employees were screaming, even though he could hear shouts and screams in the distance. They also weren't moving. Were they already dead? He didn't see much in the way of blood until he spotted a security guard slumped against a shave ice stand, his blood-soaked chest shredded.

You fuckers.

James emptied his .45 into the enemy, each ripper monster gaining a new hole in the head or the chest as he put them down. He slapped a new magazine in and frowned. Because of the time limitations he hadn't had access to his full armory, only his emergency supplies in the truck—in this case a tactical vest, along with a combat knife, a few extra magazines, and a small number of grenades. The supplies also included healing potions for himself and a spare one for humans, and since he always carried one anyway these days, that meant two for him, but that would be more than enough in normal circumstances.

I'm probably gonna need advanced mode to finish every Council asshole off.

Insufficient energy for advanced transformation, Whispy Doom noted.

James rushed over to one of the victims, a duck man in some sort of naval uniform. He blinked once he looked down. He assumed the anthropomorphic duck was one of the employees in a costume, but now that he was close, he could see the exposed circuitry. Just a mindless robot. Quick checks of the other downed characters confirmed the same. The stupid Council monsters had wasted time killing machines, meaning there was only one real victim in the square.

He glanced again at the dead security guard, then noticed the man's chest was still rising and falling James hurried to the victim and pulled out his human healing potion.

If I die later, pal, you better name your kid after me.

James forced the man's mouth open and poured the potion down this throat, watching and waiting. Thirty seconds later, his wounds closed, the security guard's eyes flickered open, and he shot up, eyeing the bounty hunter with suspicion.

"When you die, the first person you see in Heaven is James Brownstone?" the man asked. "Or, shit...am I in Hell?"

James grunted. "I'm not dead, so why would I be in Heaven or Hell?" He pointed in the general direction of the front gate. "I've got teams sweeping the park, starting from the front. It'll be safe as long as you head that way."

The security guard nodded. He glanced down at his shredded shirt and ran a hand along his unmarred body. "I thought...they killed me. You used magic?"

"Something like that," James rumbled. "Now get the fuck going,"

The guard sprinted away.

James frowned and stood. He and his teams needed to hurry up before more people got hurt. After a quick check to confirm the enemies had stayed dead, he jogged toward the source of the hum.

He winced as he came up to a decapitated rabbit character sitting in a pool of black and blue fluid. Even though he knew it was nothing more than a robot, there was something very unsettling about seeing the headless mascot.

The humming grew louder, and reddish light shone from around a nearby building, the Hall of the Perky Penguins.

Wonder if Alison would like this? Nah, she's too old. Glad I never bought those season tickets I was thinking about when she first moved in.

James grunted and ran toward the hum. He turned the corner to find a swirling portal, along with a half-dozen more eyeless rippers. Two more emerged from the portal and they all turned toward him, raising their claws and hunching.

He holstered his pistol and pulled out his knife. "Bring it, assholes. You're not so fucking tough. If you were, you wouldn't be attacking an amusement park like a bunch of pussies. Should have just come at me."

The rippers loped toward him, and James bellowed out a challenge and charged. He slammed a boot into one. It flew, and its head crunched against the brick wall of the Hall of Perky Penguins. A slash of his knife took out most of the neck of another.

Gunshots echoed in the far distance from multiple directions. The other teams were engaging their own monsters or wizards.

Several rippers surrounded James and slashed at him with their claws. They shredded his clothes and the blows stung, but the attacks only left scratches.

Near maximum adaptation previously achieved for attack, Whispy Doom reported. *Kill enemies. Find stronger enemies.*

James smashed a ripper's head into the ground with a free hand, enjoying the satisfying crunch.

Working on it, Whispy.

James slammed his elbow into one right behind him before stabbing another. The creatures continued their efforts, but blow after blow from James ended their sad, twisted lives until a tangle of bloodied bodies with twitching limbs was all that surrounded him. The only thing they'd accomplished was adding new holes to his shirt.

Two more rippers emerged from the portal. He rushed toward them and finished them with two quick stabs to the head.

James grunted and looked at the portal. Two energy streams were still feeding into it, but their sources weren't nearby.

Need to shut this shit down, or it'll just be Whack-a-Mole forever.

He sprinted away, following one of the streams. Glancing over his shoulder, he spotted more rippers emerging from the portal, but they didn't rush for him. Maybe he had to be closer for them to sense him.

James ignored the creatures. He could come back and kill them later. The most important step of the mission would be to cut down on reinforcements. He focused on following the energy stream until he found the source, a rock with a pulsing crimson energy field.

Sample energy for adaptation, Whispy Doom demanded. *Adapt. Grow stronger.*

James was about to argue with the amulet but shrugged and sheathed his knife. "Why the fuck not? Just more Council shit. I've already adapted to most of it anyway, and don't even have to kill anyone."

He touched the energy stream and pure pain burned through him. His body jerked and flew back several yards. It wasn't until he landed that he realized his hand had been vaporized.

A long hiss followed.

James grunted and tried sitting up, the pain blinding and darkness clawing at the edges of his vision.

Well, shit. That's a new one.

A flickering thought of using Alison's wish passed through his mind, but he pushed it away. It wasn't his. It was his daughter's, and he wouldn't waste it because he'd let a little mistake almost get the better of him. Besides, Whispy Doom liked to talk a good game. Time for him to help when it didn't come to combat.

The good news was the wound had been cauterized. At least he wouldn't bleed out even if he passed out.

Do something, James demanded. *If I pass out here, some damn Council asshole might be able to take me out.*

Insufficient time for regeneration, Whispy Doom responded. *Recommend supplemental healing via external means. Combination should be sufficient for limb recovery.*

Gritting his teeth and trying to push the pain out of his mind, James took several deep breaths and fished out one of his healing potions. He downed it and waited, unsure if it'd work. He'd had fingers cut off before and managed to hold them in place while a healing potion worked, but not full limb regeneration. If this didn't work, there would be a very expensive visit to a witch or wizard in his future.

The pain began to fade. Silver-green metallic tendrils, the same as with his armor, extended from the burned stub. They shifted color, turning white and forming layers of bone. Over the course of a minute the bones of his hand regenerated, then the layer of muscle, then his skin to form a completely new hand.

James flexed his new hand. No pain at all. He found himself surprised, and far less angry than he'd been only a couple minutes before. Not only was he less angry, but he was also fascinated. The potential combat implications of what he'd just done weren't lost on him at all, even if he only had one more healing potion for the job. He'd need to be a bit more careful.

Could you do that shit without the potion?

Limb regeneration possible, Whispy replied, *but energy- and time-intensive.*

Good to know, not that I'm planning to let more assholes cut me up or touch shit like that. Please tell me you're adapted to that energy at least. The fuckers might blast it at me.

Partial adaptation achieved. Additional exposure not recommended in current tactical situation.

James snorted. He pulled out his gun and fired a few rounds at the rock. They struck and bounced off with sparks, the pulsating stream unaffected by the attack.

"Fuck."

Any ideas?

Insufficient power for advanced mode.

James yanked a grenade off his vest. If he didn't have his armor blade or armor cannons, this might be the next best option. He pulled the pin and threw it toward the rock. It exploded and the stream vanished, even though the rock only looked charred.

"Good enough," he muttered.

He grinned and cracked his knuckles. With Heather disrupting the communications at his request and no way to see the other portals from where he was, he could only hope the other teams figured it out.

James turned to verify the collapse of the closest portal. Although there was no portal in the distance or even the second energy stream anymore, a group of twenty rippers slowly circled him, preparing for an assault.

Guess I took too long to blow that shit up.

After getting his hand burned off and regenerating it, a pack of monsters who couldn't do more than tear up his clothes didn't worry him at all. He holstered his pistol and readied his knife.

Kill enemies, the amulet admonished. *Find stronger enemies to maximize adaptation. Achieve primary directive.*

James grunted. Thanks to his amulet, he'd burned off his hand. Sure, it had grown back, but the damned amulet was only worried about finding new sources of damage to adapt to. Not even a little "Sorry about that, man, I gave you bad fucking advice."

The bounty hunter snorted. There would be time to worry about that later. He threw himself into the pack of rippers, becoming a whirlwind of death. Although the enemy attack finished off the ragged remains of what passed for his shirt, they paid for it with their lives.

James wiped his bloodied knife on his pants. "At least one portal down."

CHAPTER TWENTY-ONE

More insect men scampered toward Trey's team, the sun glinting off their dark carapaces and their massive mandibles clacking together. He couldn't help but be unnerved by their still-human-looking eyes.

"Why can't these fuckers just use normal-ass guys?" Trey shouted as he put a bullet into the head of one of the charging creatures. At least the damned monsters didn't require an anti-magic bullet to put down. A pile of dead monsters covered the path to the Castle of the Dream Princess. He'd love to see a few shots of that scene on the advertisements for the park.

Lachlan slapped in a new magazine and shook his head. "We took out the first portal. Just need to find the second and then we won't have to do as much fucking pest control."

The other men grunted in agreement.

Several high-pitched screams cut through the air.

Shit. There are still normal people in the park? Guess you can't empty out that many people and not have a few left behind. Time to prove how badass the Brownstone Agency is.

They sounded like they were coming from the castle, a three-story structure with a façade that resembled an ornate Renaissance-era castle, including multiple turreted towers with balconies. The team rushed toward the castle, hopping over the ropes and stanchions.

A man in a robe stood near the front of the castle, his clear wand glowing bright green. He spun toward the bounty hunters, frowning, and flung out his wand. A thick green liquid appeared and flew toward the men.

"What the fuck is that goo?" Trey shouted and jumped out of the way. The liquid coated one of the ropes near him, hissing and burning through it on contact. It was a deadly acid, and he doubted the anti-magic deflector would save them. They'd learned that the hard way when dealing with the Council before.

Lachlan yelped when some of the acid landed on his armor and started eating through it.

Trey fired a burst at the wizard, but the bullets jerked up at the last second without a flash. "Just yank that shit off, Lachlan. Everyone else, take cover before this bitch burns our dicks off."

The five bounty hunters rushed for trees, corners, and even a churro cart. The wizard kept flinging acid, the acrid smell filling the air and dissolving everything it touched. It even etched several inches into the pavement.

Lachlan rolled behind a wall, hissing as he singed his thumb but managing to get his chest armor off. "I'm okay,

Trey. Just gonna take a long fucking shower after all this shit is over, you know what I'm saying?"

The other men peppered the wizard with bullets, but every bullet changed course at the last second, not even coming close to messing up his robe let alone wounding him. That was the problem with wizards. A man could never know what kind of defensive magic one of the bastards might have.

More high-pitched screams came from inside, and Trey gritted his teeth. There was obviously somebody in the castle, so he needed that wizard to hurry up and die. He'd been trying to preserve some of his specialty ammunition, but he had no choice if they were going to save the people in the castle.

Trey ejected his magazine and slapped in anti-magic rounds.

"Time for an expensive death, motherfucker." Trey flipped the rifle to automatic and spun around the corner, holding down the trigger.

The first few bullets went wide but at least didn't abruptly change course like all the shots before had. The next few peppered the wizard, and he yelled, collapsing to his knees, blood blossoming from his wounds. Trey let go of the trigger and yanked out his pistol, letting the rifle dangle from the shoulder strap. Might as well make the coup de grace a little more cost-efficient for the agency.

He opened up with the 9mm, yelling as he emptied the magazine. The first half of his shots refused to go anywhere near the wounded wizard, but the last few slammed into the man, blowing new holes in him until he collapsed to the ground.

Trey snorted. The man had magical powers and chose to use them to try to murder people in an amusement park as part of some crazy cabal's plans.

"What a dumbass motherfucker."

Several rifle shots rang out, and Trey jerked his head to the side. Lachlan and two others had taken out a charging insect-man pack.

Damn. Lucky they were watching our ass. We could have gotten torn up.

Trey holstered his pistol and brought his rifle back up. "We still need to find that other portal or those damn bitches will keep coming at us, but let's clear the castle first."

He jogged past the body of the wizard toward the castle. Half the room was coated in acid, a ticket counter was melted in the middle, and a life-size princess robot lay on the ground, its face a twisted mass of burned metal and plastic.

"Yeah, this ain't every kid's worst nightmare. Not at all. Damn, are the Council fucked-up bitches or what?"

An insect man clawed at a metal door marked PRINCESSES AND KNIGHTS ONLY, seemingly ignoring Trey as it gouged the metal with its hard claws. A single anti-magic bullet to the head finished the monster. Another metal door had already been burned open but there was no one inside.

With the monster dead, Trey could make out quiet sobbing from the other side. He hurried to the door and knocked once, rewarded by several high-pitched screams.

"Yo," Trey shouted. "I ain't no monster. I'm Trey

Garfield. We took out the monsters and the wizard. I'm here to rescue you."

"Y-you're a normal person?" called back a voice. It sounded like a young girl's voice.

Trey frowned. "Yeah. We're the good guys, and we just killed the monsters. Like knights, y'all, just with big-ass guns and a lot more style."

The locks clicked, and the door slowly opened, revealing four young girls and two boys. They couldn't have been more than ten years old. Three of the girls wore brightly colored princess dresses, and the boys and the remaining girl had on some sort of faux shiny knight's armor costumes, complete with dull metal swords. One boy's sword had been half-melted by acid.

Bravery's only gonna get you so far, kid.

Trey nodded toward the door. "We'll get you out of here."

The kids wiped their tears and followed Trey as he led them out a side door. They didn't need to see the bullet-riddled wizard, although all the dead monsters probably weren't helping. The kids screamed as a few more rifle shots echoed nearby.

Damn. Need to get these kids somewhere safe.

The bounty hunters would run out of ammo if they didn't do something about the remaining gate, but it wasn't like Trey could just leave a group of young kids to fend for themselves. A single insect man could take them out with ease.

"Yo, Lachlan," he called. "Get your ass over here."

The other man rushed over to him, eyeing the kids.

"Damn, that was what they were going after in there? That's messed up."

Trey gave him a grim nod. "Take these kids to the front and out of the park. Just stick to the way we came and you shouldn't even run into anything. Easiest job all day."

Lachlan frowned. "But the big man said this was search and des—"

"I need you to get these kids the hell out of here." Trey glared at him. "This ain't just search-and-destroy when we've got people still in here, especially kids, you know what I'm saying? Get them out of here. Now."

Lachlan nodded and gestured with his arms. "Come on. Uncle Lachlan and his big-ass rifle are gonna save you today, kids."

One of the girls in a princess costume blinked. "Are you soldiers?"

Lachlan shook his head. "Nah, we are bounty hunters with the Brownstone Agency."

Her eyes widened. "I don't want to be a princess anymore when I grow up. I want to be a bounty hunter."

Lachlan grinned. "Just learn to kick ass, and we'll hire you. Let's go."

Trey waited until Lachlan and the kids were a good hundred yards away before nodding to the rest of his men. "Seems like the new insect bastards keep coming from the same direction. Let's go finish off the last portal and show them who the real monsters are."

Rippers and insect men loped toward Maria's team in a

tightly packed cluster. Too many years with the AET had removed her fear of monsters who could fall to conventional rounds, especially when they were acting like rabid animals and lacked strategy.

How many more of you are there?

Her team members had their rifles ready, sweat pouring down their sides as the monsters closed.

"Maintain the inverted wedge formation," Maria yelled. "Wait for it. Wait for it. *Now*. Open fire!"

The five-member team shot several quick bursts almost as one. Their bullets cut down the horde of charging rippers and insect men, who fell together in a final dance of death. The few that survived the initials bursts were shredded by the combined follow-up fire.

"Cease fire. Cease fire." Maria surveyed the carnage. Another fifteen monsters dead. There couldn't be many of the bastards left. She swore she'd killed fewer monsters when they'd raided the Council base, even if the monsters there were admittedly tougher.

Maria had to give the Brownstone boys credit. She hadn't encountered many non-AET types who could handle monsters charging right toward them and not want to break and run. It didn't matter if a person could shoot and kill one with a gun or not, unnatural mutants spoke to a person's instinct to flee. The average man couldn't even stand and fight when a normal wild animal was rushing him.

Carl slapped in a new magazine. "Starting to run low on ammo, Maria, and you told us to save our last grenades for the portals. Got a few 9mm magazines, but I'm not down with getting close enough that I have to use that shit."

The other men nodded, being in similar situations.

Maria sighed. One wounded man would destroy morale. "We've already taken out the two portals in this area. There can't be many more of the monsters left around here."

A gunshot rang out in the distance. It didn't sound like the rifles or 9mm pistols used by most of the Brownstone Agency, nor James' .45. If she had to guess, she'd say it was a .38.

Maria gestured with her arm. "Maintain the formation and let's go to where the action is. Sounds like we're not the only party in town.

Her heart pounded as they ran through a faux goblin village. Shredded goblin robots lay all over, along with several dead monsters including a few four-armed Zain, along with rippers. Fantasy had met reality, but she hadn't seen any human or Oriceran bodies.

Maria wrinkled her nose at the dead Zain. "Thought we'd seen the last of those four-armed bastards in Wyoming."

Another gunshot rang out.

"Why is another team in Fantasyville?" Carl puffed beside her. "They already finish up in Robotown?"

Maria shook her head. "Listen to the shots. I don't think they are with the agency. Whoever they are, we've got to help them."

The edge of goblin village gave way to the Tree City of the Forest Elves, a large sign in front informing all visitors that "This fun zone is based purely on fictional depictions of elves, and no resemblance to living elves, whether from

Earth or Oriceran, is intended" followed by another sign reading "California Proposition 65 Warning: Detectable amounts of chemicals known to cause cancer, birth defects, or other reproductive harm are found in and around this exhibit."

Maria snickered. The whole park was littered with signs like that. Then again, so were large chunks of California, as if they thought everyone was going to drop dead from cancer any second if they sipped coffee or visited an amusement park.

Everyone's always worried about the tiny risks and not the big ones like crime, car accidents, or weird-ass monsters trying to eat your face.

Maria led her team around the trunk of a fake treehouse and spotted several dead rippers around the base of a tall living tree with an observing platform about twenty feet up. Two men in uniform, security guards from what she could tell, stood at the top, pistols in hand, blood caked on their faces.

More guys with balls. Good for them.

Two Zain clawed furiously at the trunk of the tree, ripping out bark and wood, a pile forming around them. The men had no angle on the monsters from the platform.

"Take the bastards out," Maria shouted, aiming her rifle.

The four men and the woman fired almost simultaneously, the bullets ripping into the two Zain. The creatures spun and charged the V-formation, taking two more volleys before stumbling to the ground, dead.

Maria stepped forward and swept the area with her rifle. The Council monsters might not be too bright, but they'd already run into a wizard. She glanced down at her darkened deflector. If they hadn't been wearing their deflectors, they'd probably be dead.

"Carl and Deshawn, watch our backs," she ordered. She jogged over to the tree. "What the hell are you still doing here? Didn't you hear you were supposed to evacuate?"

One of the guards shrugged. "We thought we could maybe slow some of the monsters down so the visitors would have a better chance of getting away. Are any more of them coming?"

Maria shook her head. "We've taken out the feeder portals in this area. Just head back to the main plaza directly from here, and you'll be fine." She grinned up at them. "If we don't all die during this, I know an agency that can use some brave men and probably pays better than this place." She turned back to the bounty hunters. "We should go and reinforce Max's team in Robotown. Let's get back into formation and sweep that way. If they're fine, we can continue sweeping to the next zone until we've cleared this entire damned park."

"Maria, look out!" Carl shouted.

She spun just in time to see a wizard shimmer into existence, his wand crackling with energy and pointed right at her. Her pulse sped up, and she raised her rifle. A full blast at this range might take her out, especially with her already-weakened deflector.

A gunshot rang out and the wizard collapsed to the ground with a hole in his head, his wand falling and the energy dissipating harmlessly.

Maria let out a sigh of relief and turned to give Carl a grin. "Thanks. You saved my ass there."

He shook his head. "I couldn't take the shot. You were in the way. I couldn't risk it."

She furrowed her brow. "Then who?"

"Me," called a familiar voice from her side.

Maria turned.

Shay stood there, her 9mm in hand and a huge grin on her face. "Looks like this time I had *your* back, Maria."

CHAPTER TWENTY-TWO

"Can't these bastards just give up already?" James rumbled.

He grunted as his grenade finished off the energy stream to the second portal in Animal Town, then pulled out his gun and tried to decide his next move. He was closer to Princess Island, so it made more sense to head that way. The gunfire from across the park had grown sparser, so either his teams were winning and the incident was almost over, or he'd have to figure out another way to close the portals without grenades.

"The great James Brownstone," rasped a voice from behind.

James spun and raised his gun. A swirling cloud of red mist floated several yards behind him, wispy tendrils flowing from its sides. It had two glowing red eyes atop a bulge that he supposed was its head. He recognized the bastard from footage Senator Johnston had supplied him.

"So you're not dead, He Who Hunts," James rumbled.

"I'm not lying when I say I'm surprised. Given that you haven't been around, I figured you had to be dead and not just hiding."

Kill stronger enemy, the amulet whispered in his mind. *Adapt. Grow stronger. Achieve primary directive.*

The creature let out a low chuckle. "Did you think your feeble soldier friends could kill me?" He floated up a few feet, his tendrils twitching. "I am beyond perishing at the hands of such pathetic creatures."

James snorted. "Why? Seems like we're killing all your little Council bitches easily enough, not to mention your friends."

He Who Hunts floated even higher. "The others were disposable. The minions are disposable. You're proud of all my minions you've slain?"

James gave a slight shrug. "Yeah. I was expecting a tougher fight, but you might as well have brought some paper dolls the way I've been cutting through them."

Another rasping chuckle followed. "Perfect. Where do you think I got most of these creatures, James Brownstone?"

James shrugged. "I don't know. Some fucking evil version of Costco on Oriceran?"

He Who Hunts floated back closer to the ground. "No. All people I've taken from this sad little planet. I've taken pathetic humans and twisted them, warped them, ripped out their souls to make them nothing more than my puppets, to throw them against you and your minions."

James' face twitched and he gritted his teeth, heart pounding. "What the fuck?"

"Yes, you *should* feel the rage. The anger. If it makes you feel any better, there was nothing that could have been done to save them. Once I reshaped them, they would never again be anything but my servants. They would have died in days if you hadn't slain them. I only needed them here to sow terror."

Yes, the amulet sent. *Anger. Hatred. Power increasing.*

This shit ends today, no matter what.

James opened fire, pulling the trigger until his gun clicked empty. No ichor spilled from He Who Hunts. Each bullet melted into vapor on contact, and unlike his encounter with the wizards outside the barbeque place, the Council member wasn't wounded by the secondary vapor.

"Pathetic," He Who Hunts rasped. "Disappointing. It was difficult, don't you understand? I was forced to be cautious as I harvested your kind to turn into my minions, and this is all you can do? Fling metal at me? I was expecting something far more impressive. I've seen it— your true second skin. Your true power. Was it all just temporary? A bargain to gain the power you needed to defeat the Council?"

"Fuck you." James ground his teeth together. Senator Johnston had told him soldiers had been able to wound He Who Hunts, but without anti-magic bullets, maybe he had no chance. There was no way he could let the bastard go after everything he had done. Not only that, he still owed him for his men damaging the barbeque restaurant.

Give me advanced mode, James demanded.

Insufficient power for advanced mode.

James holstered his pistol. "If you're so fucking tough, take me out. Because you're dying today, you piece of shit. I don't care what you are. I know you can bleed. I know you can *die*, because you've been hiding like a little fucking cockroach this entire time while you sent wizards or those twisted people after me." He sneered. "You're nothing, are you?"

He Who Hunts flicked up a tendril and a red energy bolt slammed into James' already-bare chest, a wave of heat passing over him. He hissed in pain and stumbled back a few feet.

After taking a deep breath, he looked down. Even though the wound throbbed, he had only a light burn.

Additional adaptation achieved, Whispy Doom crowed, his joy infectious. *Kill enemy. Grow stronger.*

James' hand dropped to his knife, but he didn't pull it out. He doubted he could stab a flying mist cloud to death, not without one of Shay's magical blades at least. No reason to melt a perfectly good knife.

James snorted. "That all you got? You're supposed to be the big bad last member of the Council, and you can't kill me?" He slapped his chest. "Come on, asshole. Prove to me how scary you are."

He Who Hunts' tendrils twitched a few times. "Interesting. I'd wondered if this was all a waste, but you're not dead. Still, you're not what you should be, either. You remain a disappointment. I might not be able to kill you, but you can do little to harm me with your sad toys."

"Fuck you. The longer you sit here, the sooner my guys come, and you're dead then. Or you gonna run and hide?" James grinned at him. "I owe you for sending those guys who blew up Phillips-Bar-B-Que. You should have just floated back to Oriceran and learned your fucking lesson, asshole. But you're stubborn, just like the fucking Harriken, and you're gonna join them in Hell."

He Who Hunts flung another heat bolt at James. "Your arrogance is glorious, Brownstone. Myopic, but glorious."

The magical attack stung, but only reddened James' skin this time. The Council member pelted him with a few other attacks, burning a hole in his pants but not doing much tissue damage. Even the pain from the light burn from the first attack already seemed to be fading. His amulet's newly-developed enhanced healing and defenses were keeping him in the fight, but no man could win a fight only by taking hits.

James let out a low growl. Even though he hated the monster in front of him, the kind of boiling rage he needed just wasn't pouring out.

Insufficient power for advanced transformation, Whispy complained. *Near maximum adaptation achieved. Kill enemy.*

The amulet radiated faint disappointment.

James cracked his knuckles. He needed to get mad. The lingering fire from realizing where the Council member had gathered his forces kept calmness away, but it wasn't enough.

Why the fuck can't I get mad enough? Never thought I'd regret having such good control of my fucking emotions.

James grunted and shook his head. "No matter what I have to do or who I have to pay, even if you escape today, I'll find you, and I will make sure that you die. Do you fucking understand me?"

He Who Hunts floated back a few feet. "Yes," he rasped. "You're the one I need. I'm impressed you were able to stop my massacre, but your efforts will accomplish nothing.

The sickening order must perish. Chaos must reign. Today is just the first of many massacres I will deliver. I will reduce this city to nothing but ash, bone, and blood because you can't stop me."

James snorted. "Fuck off, asshole. You're not exactly hurting me either."

He Who Hunts let out a long hollow laugh. "Doesn't it bother you, Brownstone? Serving inferiors? Insects beneath you? Tools of static corruption?"

James narrowed his eyes. "What the fuck are you going on about now, you misty piece of shit?"

"You protect these people? Why?" He Who Hunts flung a tentacle to the side. A heat bolt shot out and incinerated a nearby sign, reducing it to molten slag. "Billions of humans. Even if you killed ninety-nine percent of them, there would still be millions. Are their lives so valuable? Why do you care? They are beneath you."

"This isn't Red Mist World, fucker. This is Earth." James slammed a fist into his palm. "And we don't take kindly to genocidal fucking maniacs regardless of what species they are."

The Council member floated up several feet. "If you served me, I would free you from fear, from doubt, from anything that would distract from your instincts. Revel in pure instincts. Revel in the natural order of chaos."

James snorted. "Spare me. I'm not looking for a new king or a new god."

Where the fuck is everybody else? I'm sure we can at least light this asshole up with anti-magic bullets. I hope they have some left.

James whipped out his .45, slapped in a new magazine,

and emptied it again into his opponent, but the shots still didn't do any good. With a grunt, he holstered the weapon.

"That's your answer?" He Who Hunts asked. "Pointless defiance? I thought the Council members were foolish, but you're beyond that."

James charged He Who Hunts and threw a punch. The creature didn't dodge. His fist passed right through, the mist spilling out. He hissed at the heat of the contact and stumbled a few feet away, shaking out his fist. His skin was reddened, but the mist had already poured back into He Who Hunts. Another stalemate.

He needed a better strategy. The damned Council member might portal out any second and then there was no telling when they might catch him.

James' blood ran cold at a sudden bark. His dog was charging into the area, the leash trailing behind him. It'd been chewed through.

Oh, shit.

The dog kept rushing toward He Who Hunts, barking and growling. Justice instincts.

He Who Hunts' tendrils lifted and a shuddering red sphere of energy grew between them. "What an insolent creature. Let's erase it."

The energy screamed through the air.

CHAPTER TWENTY-THREE

No. Not again.

James was too far away to get to the dog and take the shot. "To me, boy," he shouted.

The dog changed course, sprinting toward James. The last-second move let it dodge a direct hit from the energy ball. He Who Hunts' magic exploded right behind the dog, flinging the singed and yelping animal through the air. The dog hit the ground and rolled, still breathing but whimpering.

"You piece of shit," James growled. "This is your great instinct? Your great fucking chaos?"

It was nothing but pointless cruelty from a monster who'd twisted and murdered dozens, if not hundreds, of people. Maybe thousands, for all James knew. Another small piece to push him over the edge.

"It survived," rasped He Who Hunts. "Impressive. Caring about this creature is even more pointless. Sentiment is false order. You begin to bore me, Brownstone. Are you the same being who defeated the soul-drinkers?"

James trembled in rage, his heart thundering and blood pounding in his ears. His hands curled into fists as he stomped toward He Who Hunts. "I…will…fucking…*end*…you," he growled.

He Who Hunts brightened. "Interesting."

Yessss! Anger. Hatred. Sufficient power for extended advanced transformation, Whispy reported.

Silver-green tendrils poured from the amulet, spreading and flattening into armor that encased first his chest, then his arms, and legs. The armor covered his hands, and claws extended, followed by a blade out of each arm. A helmet sealed around his head, and his eyes ached for a moment before he could see again, but as before, he had wider peripheral vision.

James let out a low growl.

Extended advanced transformation achieved. Kill the enemy. Grow stronger. Achieve primary directive. Additional adaptation minimal from current enemy.

Heavy footfalls sounded behind him, and with his improved peripheral vision, he spotted Shay, Maria, Trey, and the rest of the men closing on him. He stepped toward He Who Hunts, ignoring the arrivals even as their rifles came to life. Their bullets vaporized and did no damage, just like his.

"You wanted the man who fought those monsters in Wyoming," James shouted. "Here I fucking am, fucker."

He Who Hunts laughed and zoomed away and James charged after him.

You don't fucking get away, you bastard. If you want to

leave, you better portal right now.

The Council member tossed several more heat bolts behind him. They struck the armor, but James barely felt the hits. He Who Hunts kept ascending. After the fourth hit, he stopped attacking.

James jumped and swung his blade but missed. The damned bastard was now straight-up flying. The creature rushed toward a nearby roller coaster, the bounty hunter stomping after him, growling and snarling.

He Who Hunts stopped in front of the bottom track of the roller coaster near the loading zone but hovered thirty feet in the air. "You can't win. You're pathetic, Brownstone. You can't protect anyone, not even a single lesser beast." He floated up with a raspy chuckle as he headed toward the top of a nearby loop.

Make me fly, James demanded.

Not a viable adaptation, Whispy demanded. *Implementing viable alternative.*

Pain shot through James' legs, and he hissed. It passed a moment later, but even with the rage running through his mind, he understood what had happened.

He bent down and jumped, flinging himself into the air. It might not have been flight, but he was rushing right toward his target, one of his blades raised high.

The Council member jerked to the side, and James missed, his blade slicing through a support beam instead.

James fell to the ground, landing with a loud thud. He stood, turned, and sought his foe. The crack of gunshots filled the air as his friends continued their assault. A distant corner of his mind remembered they had anti-magic bullets, and he couldn't understand why He Who Hunts wasn't bleeding.

The mist entity spun toward the bounty hunters and blasted several heat bolts their way, forcing them to scatter for cover. James took advantage of his distraction to leap again, this time getting closer to the enemy but still missing his flying foe. Jumping, even super-jumping, wasn't a match for true flight.

He crashed into a turn in the tracks, bending the metal. With a grunt, he stood, glaring at He Who Hunts

"You fucking cockroach," James screamed. "Stop running."

His amulet's euphoria filled the back of his mind as he drank in his anger and hatred.

He concentrated for a moment. Green light flowed and twisted over the blades, his energy cannons charging with a crackle and hiss. A few seconds later, he shot two blasts. The rays narrowly missed the quick-moving Council member, but they blew through a track on the other side, incinerating it.

His friends stopped firing to watch in stunned silence but he ignored them, charging and firing again and again at the juking He Who Hunts. None of his blasts landed, but several carved through support beams or the tracks of the roller coaster, which now groaned and shuddered under its weight.

Warning, Whispy Doom reported, some of his euphoria fading, *power level may be insufficient for continued energy attacks.*

You wanted me pissed and angry. Now I fucking am. I'll shoot as much as I fucking want.

James leapt to the highest point on the tracks, taking another shot while he was in the air, but his beams blasted into the ground, sending up a cloud of dirt and rock but still not wounding his enemy. He let out a loud growl.

He Who Hunts cut to the side and zigzagged toward James, firing several bright red bolts. James hissed, ready to take the shots, realizing too late that his enemy wasn't firing at him but at the support structures below him.

The blasts vaporized the already weakened and strained structure, and the metal screeched and groaned before a loud crack echoed around James. The support beams snapped in succession, the entirety of the elevated tracks dropping. James stumbled, falling straight down without anywhere to push off. He tumbled to the ground, taking his last few seconds to fire another blast at He Who Hunts.

This shit's not gonna stop me.

One of the rays nailed the creature's side, an unearthly dissonant buzz filled the air, and a shower of green ichor rained from He Who Hunts' wound. The Council member fell straight toward the ground.

James' mix of rage and satisfaction disappeared as he slammed into a pile of wood. Despite falling hundreds of feet and landing hard, he barely felt the impact. Whatever pain should have accompanied such an epic trip was blocked by his armor and his rage. He rolled onto his back just in time to be buried under a multi-ton shower of wood and steel.

Darkness swallowed his vision and he thrashed, unable to move.

No. I need to make sure he's dead. No!

James' arms were pinned, and he grunted and strained

to move them to no avail. He let out a loud growl and fired a single energy blast, clearing some of the rubble near his right arm. This allowed him to change his arm's direction and shoot in front of him. Other rubble collapsed on top of him, but now a few rays of light cut through the darkness.

Warning. Power levels may be insufficient for sustained energy attacks.

Almost all the amulet's euphoria had vanished.

His rage-clouded mind ignored the amulet as he managed to get his arm pointing forward and fired another blast. Bits of metal and dirt rained down on him, but now he could clearly see his path to the surface. With a yell, he yanked out his other arm and began shoving and slicing obstacles on his way out of the remains of the rollercoaster.

He needed to get to the target. He needed to *kill* the target. James emerged from the pile of rubble and looked around, seeking the wounded He Who Hunts.

The Council member floated only a foot above a small pool of glowing green ichor, a semi-translucent dome surrounding him. A few smashed bullets in front of him proved the team had already tried to shoot him while James was digging himself out.

"I'm going to fucking kill you," James roared.

At the edge of his vision, Shay was gesturing to the others to pull back. They did so, splitting their attention between James and his enemy.

Three ribbons of solid crimson energy like tears in space itself appeared within the dome. Red mist began pouring out of the tears and flowing into He Who Hunts. He began to inflate, his body rapidly filling the dome, which vanished a second later. No more ichor dripped from his side, and soon he was gargantuan, an evil storm cloud, his terrible eyes like twin red suns. Dozens of misty tendrils now extended from the red mass.

The Brownstone team opened fire again, but their bullets didn't do any damage.

James leapt away from his would-be grave and landed a few yards from his enemy. He let out a long, low growl. "Just fucking *die* already."

He Who Hunts let out a hollow laugh and a spinning red crystal appeared above him, wisps and arcs of energy surrounding and connecting to his tendrils.

"It's time, Brownstone," He Who Hunts announced. "Now that you've finally reached a proper state, you will become a slave to chaos. You will become my tool."

"I will fucking rip you apart," James howled. He snapped his arms up and prepared to fire again. At this range, there was no way he could miss something that large.

A few seconds passed before he realized his mind was too quiet. Even when Whispy Doom wasn't saying anything. The amulet's feelings, particularly his bloodlust, were always there, seeping into James' mind, but now there was nothing. His thoughts were as quiet as when he wasn't bonded.

Pain spiked through James' head, and he shook it. The pain intensified, and he fell to his knees. The rage in his mind twisted in on itself in a loop, but his thoughts started blanking. He couldn't remember who he was fighting or why.

He Who Hunts floated closer. Energy arced from the

red crystal into the armor. "You've not reached your true potential. I can taste it. You've not reached it by far. Crude. Weak, because of your pathetic mind. Your pathetic soul. I will wield you as the weapon you were meant to be."

Whispy? Can't...think. Do...something. Where...am...I?

No response.

He Who Hunts glowed brighter. "You're a dull blade, Brownstone. You will be sharpened, and I will use you to cut through the feeble lies of this planet. The false order. Rejoice! You are about to be repurposed into something far more useful."

His mind gone, James was distantly aware of Shay screaming and charging in, her *tachi* raised.

What? Shay...no.

"There's only one person who gets to tell him what to do, you evil piece of cloud shit," Shay shouted. "And that's me." She swung her sword into the mist. It sliced through, spilling ichor, the blade untouched.

A tendril slammed into Shay, and a white field flashed around her. She flew back, slamming into the ground and rolling several times, her sword clattering away from her hand.

NO!

James bellowed a bone-shaking roar. The new anger blasted through his mind like a cleansing fire.

Link reestablished, Whispy announced. *Initiating thought filter. Extended advanced mode power-up achieved. Kill the enemy.*

James rushed toward He Who Hunts. A tendril whipped at him, and he slashed with his blade. The tendril burst into millions of tiny floating particles and a wave of green energy accompanied the hit, shooting right through the massive red cloud forming He Who Hunts' body and showering James in his enemy's glowing ichor.

He Who Hunts glowed brighter. Several heat bolts and spheres shot from the masses of tendrils and pelted James, but they didn't do much more than scorch the armor.

Near-maximum adaptation achieved against attack type, the amulet whispered. *Enemy no longer useful. Kill enemy. Grow stronger. Achieve primary directive.*

James threw himself into the red mist, slashing and slicing, each movement summoning another energy blast. Huge chunks of the cloud blew off, holes appearing. A steady drift of red particles floated into the sky almost like red smoke. The green ichor continued to rain down, now forming glowing puddles. The red crystal remained floating above the pool.

Kill, kill, kill, Whispy chanted.

"I...may...die," He Who Hunts rasped. "But...it... doesn't...matter. You...will...become...He Who Destroys. I...sacrifice...myself...to...chaos."

Rage and hatred overtook James. He kept swinging his new energy blades, his body moving itself. Pure instinct maybe, or Whispy Doom controlling him directly—he didn't know. Didn't care. All he cared about was destroying the Council member before him. The thing that had hurt his dog. The thing that had dared wound his woman. James kept hacking for a good minute even after all the red mist was gone and only a sizzling pool of green ichor remained. The red crystal crackled with even more energy.

He let out another roar and started stabbing the pool. It wasn't good enough. The enemy hadn't suffered enough.

He would destroy him, erase every particle of the bastard that still existed.

Kill, kill, kill. Yessssss. Yes. No. No. No. Warning. Thought filter failing. Initiat—

Agony shot through James' head, and he fell to his knees. Images of Father Thomas, Leeroy, Shay, and Alison dead flashed through his head like a horrific slideshow. He saw Shorty dead, then Trey and others, the darkness circling in his mind.

A presence sank into his mind, whispering unintelligibly like his amulet had once done, but the words were cold, distant, and ancient. Wrong, like even hearing them seared his soul. A spinning vortex of red filled his imagination.

"James," someone called, familiar but distant.

He let out another roar, now alternating his blades and splashing the liquid remains of the Council member all over the area, the agony in his head growing.

The dark images kept repeating, speeding up. He saw himself killing his friends and loved ones. He saw them killing him.

"James," the voice called again, insistent. "Come back to me. You won. Damn it, *you won*. I'm here for you, and I love you. Whatever the fuck is going on, fight it! You only get to lose to me, and no one fucking else, you understand me?"

He spun toward the voice, ready to destroy another foe. Shay stood there, a huge hole burned through her shirt, but her wounds were gone. His dog stood beside her, his head cocked to the side in confusion.

No, no, NO!

James growled and turned. The red crystal pulsed now, each pulse bringing new pain.

He leapt into the air and brought one of his blades down on it. His blade sliced through and the crystal exploded, the fireball engulfing him and blowing a hole in his chest armor. He crashed into the ground, every part of his body hurting, but at least the pain in his head and the dark images were gone.

Link reestablished, Whispy sent. *Severe damage sustained. Time needed for adaptation and regeneration. Recommend external healing. Entering quiescence to preserve function.*

The armor retracted and James groaned, barely able to keep his eyes open.

Shay rushed over to him, the dog at her side. The dog licked James' face as his girlfriend knelt beside him and pulled out his last healing potion.

"Cutting it kind of close," Shay muttered. She opened his mouth and poured the potion down his throat. "Trying to be dramatic now to impress me?"

James could only manage a groan in response.

Shay held his head as the other bounty hunters rushed to surround him. The dog kept licking his face and whimpering.

The pain ebbed and James sat up, rubbing his head. "Fuck. That shit hurt."

Shay blew out a sigh of relief. Maria and the men all grinned.

James looked at the splattered pools of ichor all over the place. "At least this time I got the fucker." He blinked at the dog. "And he's okay?"

Trey stepped forward. "Wasn't sure if a healing potion

would work on a dog, but it seems like it did." He shrugged. "Who knew?"

James grunted. Zoe needed to make special potions for him, but normal potions would work for both humans and dogs? Did that make him better or worse than a dog?

He chuckled and scratched behind his dog's ears. "You're just like me, boy. You run toward trouble no matter how fucking stupid it is."

The dog barked and wagged his tail.

CHAPTER TWENTY-FOUR

An hour later police swarmed the entire park, along with FBI and even a few PDA agents. Although the cops were keeping the media out, they couldn't do much about the news drones and helicopters flying overhead, all getting clear pictures of the piles of dead monsters or occasional deceased wizard in the amusement park. The previous battles against the Council had been hidden from the eyes of the public, but now the deadly group's efforts would be all over the internet with shocking photos.

Sergeant Weber shook his head as he looked at the remains of the rollercoaster and frowned at James. "The FBI and the PDA are going to have a lot of questions, but I think they want to finish up their initial investigation before they bother you. They're definitely going to come knocking in the next few days. If this was just about you taking down a few Council monsters, that's one thing, but…" He sighed and gestured to the ruins of the rollercoaster. "You destroyed a multi-million dollar rollercoaster in the process, and you didn't immediately contact the police when you knew of the threat. Some people might accuse you of caring more about the bounty than people's safety."

James shrugged. "Don't give a shit what people think. I did what I had to."

Maria stepped forward and glared at Weber, and he winced. "Are you fucking kidding me right now? He told you what happened. His informant put her life on the line." She gestured to a pile of dead rippers. "And even though Council monsters were flooding this park, there wasn't a single civilian death. That's better than even AET can achieve most of the time in situations nowhere near as bad."

Sergeant Weber put up his hands. "I'm not saying I believe that, Lieutena—"

"Maria," she corrected. "I'm not a cop anymore, and I don't have any rank. I'm just a bounty hunter with the Brownstone Agency."

Sergeant Weber sighed and shrugged. "I'm just telling you what some people think. It'll be hard to clear James entirely without his informant coming forward. People will have questions."

Maria frowned but didn't say anything else.

Shay snorted and rolled her eyes. She leaned down to pet the dog. "Yeah, that will do wonders for not getting her killed."

James grunted and shook his head. "I don't care what anyone fucking thinks. We ended the Council for good and no one who didn't have it coming died. Sounds like a fucking win to me. If the FBI and the PDA want to bust my balls, fine. I don't give a shit, and I'll just call Senator Johnston. He owes me, and he can probably get them off my back. As for the damage…" He rubbed his chin and looked at the rollercoaster debris. A group of PDA agents and CSI were inspecting the ichor pools and collecting samples. "Fuck it."

Sergeant Weber blinked. "Fuck it?"

Shay grinned. Maria nodded.

James shrugged. "This ain't barbeque or some struggling mom-and-pop restaurant. This is a major amusement park, and I'm sure they have insurance for a class-six bounty hunter taking on a magical mist monster. If I hadn't shown up a lot of people would have gotten hurt, so I'm not fucking apologizing for doing what I had to do."

Sergeant Weber rubbed the bridge of his nose. "Look, Brownstone, I'm on your side. I'm just saying the optics of this are bad, and you have to think of the public relations angles and stuff."

Maria sighed and groaned. "I hate to say it, but Weber's right, even though it pisses me off that we even have to be talking about something like this. Depending on how the brass at the LAPD and the local politicians react, they could really make trouble for you. This isn't you busting through the walls at a dust house."

James grunted. "Fine. I'll donate half my bounty money to the park as a goodwill gesture, but not the whole thing. We *earned* that fucking money."

Sergeant Weber nodded. "Okay, like I said, I'm on your side. At least the brass will be happy. I've got to go check with the CSIs and the FBI liaisons. Seriously, though, good work, Brownstone. No matter what you think, I'm on your side." He gave James a nod and walked off.

The dog barked a few times and wagged his tail.

Trey wandered over from where he'd been chatting with the other bounty hunters. "Lachlan told me those kids are all okay. Their parents have picked them up. A few scratches, but nothing serious."

"That'll be some good PR at least," Maria muttered. She glanced Weber's way before leaning toward James. "I knew you had some badass artifacts," she murmured, "but you really let yourself off the chain that time. *Damn*, Brownstone."

Shay pursed her lips and said nothing.

Trey nodded his eager agreement. "She's right. That shit was *crazy*, James. We were going to town on that mother-fucker with anti-magic bullets and they weren't scratching him, but you were fucking him up like nothing else." He pointed this thumb over his shoulder. "Overheard some PDA motherfuckers talking about He Who Hunts having sucked out a bunch of people's life forces to make himself stronger over the last few weeks or some shit like that."

James grunted. That at least explained why the military had been able to wound him but his team hadn't scratched him.

He glanced toward one of the ichor pools. "Wasn't strong enough."

Trey grinned. "Yeah, that's what I'm talking about. Pure James Motherfucking Brownstone."

Maria gave Trey a light punch in the shoulder. "Your guys weren't so bad themselves. I was thinking before I'd have to spend a lot more time with tactical training, but it's like they'd been in a SWAT or AET team for years, the way they were reacting to the situation."

"You ain't so bad yourself, Maria. I'll be straight up with you. Some of the guys wondered if you'd be all that without a railgun and shit." Trey shrugged. "But you don't need any of that crap to kick ass." He turned to James. "Do you still need anything from me, big man? I think we're all gonna head back to Camp Brownstone, clean up, and go relax after that shit. Talk about a long fucking day."

James shook his head. "Sounds good. You guys take a break. You deserve it."

Maria smiled. "Yeah. Even though I called Tyler, I think he needs to see my face to calm down. Sent me a text earlier about 'Told you so. This is what happens when you hang around Brownstone. It's only going to get worse from here.'"

Shay smirked. "Can't say he's wrong. My life used to be…simpler."

James grunted at her.

Trey and Maria waved before walking off in separate directions.

After the others were gone, Shay shot a soft smile at James. "You okay? I know you didn't feel like giving the total story to the cops. I'm still not clear what happened at the end. More suit rage?" She held up a hand. "And before you get mopey, keep in mind we needed that shit for you to win today."

James shook his head. "It's something that Council bastard was trying to do. Take my mind over or some shit with that red crystal. I couldn't hear Whispy, and it was fucking with my head." He shrugged. "Didn't matter. Because of you, it didn't take."

Shay winked. "See, James, you need me around to save your ass. Otherwise, you'd grow a beard and become the Evil James Brownstone."

"Probably." He blew out a breath. "At least now we know for certain the Council's fucking done." He frowned. "When it was screwing with me, it was making me think about everyone I care about being hurt. Bad shit in my head, even all the way back to Father Thomas." He shook his head. "But it wasn't like before in Japan. I know I'm living up to his sacrifice every day now. Maybe that's why it didn't try the same kind of shit." His eyes widened, and his gaze cut to his dog. "What about Thomas for a name?"

Shay tilted her head and shrugged. "It's a lot better than any of the other names I've heard."

James knelt and scratched behind the dog's ears. "How about you, boy? Would you like to be 'Thomas?'"

The dog barked and thumped his tail against the ground.

"I think he likes it." James smiled.

Shay shrugged. "Not too late to call him…what was the one you told me Isaiah wanted? 'Ass-kicker McGruff Brownstone?'"

"I think I'll stick with Thomas."

Shay grinned. "It's shorter anyway."

Kathy took several breaths as she polished glasses at the Black Sun. Her head still hurt from lack of sleep, but she was afraid that if she went home, the Eyes might kill her. At least in public, he might be more circumspect. It wasn't a great plan, but it *was* a plan.

Brownstone had called and told her how everything had gone down. The thought that she'd helped save thousands of lives was comforting, but that it might have cost her own wiped out all the satisfaction. She'd grown rather attached to living in her twenty-five years on the planet.

She'd thought she held up her end up the bargain, but couldn't be sure now that half the law enforcement in the county was at the amusement park. The spectral information broker might even interpret Maria as a cop. The last thing Kathy wanted to do was try to argue semantics with something so alien.

Tyler glanced her way. "This is why I don't get involved in anything unless there is money involved. A clean conscience won't pay your bills, and if you're going to die, it makes more sense to die for money than ideals." He chuckled. "I also could have told you to not make a deal like that with the Eyes."

Kathy snorted. "You also told me he was conning me and full of shit. If I hadn't sent Brownstone to that place, a lot of people would have died. I don't even know if the AET could have put down He Who Hunts."

"And what did you get out of it other than stress?" Tyler grinned. "Nothing you can spend, that's for sure."

Kathy smirked. "Oh, I forgot to tell you." She pulled out her phone and brought up her messages. She slid the phone across the bar to Tyler.

His eyes widened. "What the fuck? Am I reading this right? Where did all that money come from?"

"Brownstone. He said I should have a little reward for helping him, and since these guys were technically bounties, he gave me a piece of the action." She shrugged. "So, looks like I succeeded even on *your* terms, assuming I don't get killed by the Eyes." She snorted and picked up another glass to polish.

Her phone buzzed in Tyler's hands. He looked down at it and chuckled.

Kathy frowned. "What does it say?"

"'You pass, little girl. You still owe me one answer to a mystery, and next time the cost will be much higher.'" Tyler snorted. "That guy's so theatrical he should quit being an information broker and just get an agent already."

Kathy let out a sigh of relief. "Not going to die today anyway."

"We all die eventually, but don't worry." Tyler grinned. "You're not a real information broker until at least five different species have tried to kill you." He nodded toward the door. "You look like a necromancer's failed experiment. Go home and get some sleep. You've earned it." He shook his finger. "Not because you saved a bunch of stupid kids and their parents at that park, but because you did it and made a profit at the same time."

Kathy laughed. "Priorities."

"Always."

CHAPTER TWENTY-FIVE

The next evening Shay opened James' door and stepped into his living room. Her man was crouched next to Thomas, playing tug-of-war with an old stuffed sock. The dog growled and pulled until James released and let him have the sock with a grin.

"You'll have to do better," James rumbled.

Thomas barked a few times and dragged the sock off to his doggie bed.

James looked up at Shay. "Everything okay with Lily?"

She nodded. "Yeah, the raid went off without a hitch, and she delivered the artifact to the client. In a few years, because of all those powers, she'll make me look like a joke as a tomb raider." She let out a wistful sigh.

James stood and moved to the couch to take a seat. "Is that a bad thing?"

Shay sat beside him and shook her head. "Nope. It's just making me think about the future and shit. When I faked my death, my big master plan was nothing more than to make a shit-ton of money and retire to some island where no one would know me and try to kill me, where I'd live in seclusion for the rest of my days."

"Not a bad plan."

She shrugged. "Maybe not, but it wasn't like I was *really* thinking about the future either. I just was trying not to die. But shit happened, and everything changed."

James frowned. "Shit? Seems like things have gotten safer for you. We took out the cartel." He shrugged.

Shay nodded. "Exactly. The main people who wanted me dead are gone. I've got friends. I've effectively got two daughters, one of whom is growing up to be a tomb raider and the other probably a bounty hunter. It fills me with a sick sense of pride as a former-killer-turned-tomb-raider." She smirked and shrugged.

James grunted. "Just because we took Alison on some bounties over the summer doesn't mean she's gonna be a bounty hunter. She could do anything."

"You say that, but she was loving it toward the end." Shay shook her head. "I guarantee you that she'll end up a bounty hunter. Maybe not right away. Probably go to college to find herself or some shit first, but she's a half-Drow with a badass bounty-hunter father. It's almost inevitable." She shrugged. "It's the same reason I could never settle down to just be a professor. It's interesting, but there's a part of me that wants the rush of the challenge, just like Alison gets a rush out of taking down bad guys. She doesn't even have to pretend to not care as much as you tried to."

James rubbed the back of her neck. "I was just trying to

make sure she could defend herself. I hope I haven't fucked her up."

Shay laughed. "James, even with your super-amulet, I think Alison's eventually going to be stronger than you. In some ways, she already is. I wouldn't worry about her. I'd worry about all the poor bastards she's going after. She's got that Brownstone temper." She winked. "But that's the thing. Now I find myself worrying less about living safely on some island and more about things like what Alison's going to do in the future, or even what my big tough alien boyfriend's going to be doing a few years from now. It's less about my island and more about you and me."

"What do you mean?"

Shay sighed. "Don't know. I think I need to have a tele-porting wizard on retainer. The one time I convince myself it's okay to go away, I leave, and then I rush back to find you blowing up an amusement park."

James grunted. "Only part of it." He shrugged. "But it's not a big deal. We cleared out the last of the Council. Shit, the park wouldn't even take my donation, so it was a good payday."

"They wouldn't?" Shay arched a brow. "You didn't tell me that."

"They called when you were talking to Lily." James chuckled. "Turns out they already had 'extraordinary magic damage' insurance. They did ask me if I'd do some promotional stuff for them, maybe even be a guest for a Brownstone Day."

Shay smirked. "Really, now? And what did you tell them?"

James shrugged. "That I wasn't interested. I don't want

to sit around at some amusement park signing fucking autographs all day." He nodded at Shay. "I also don't want you thinking you need to babysit me. I'm a big boy. I don't need diapers or a nanny. Even a hot one."

"I know you can take care of yourself." Shay ran her tongue along the inside of her mouth. "Look, how about a compromise? I bet your relationship podcast is always talking about compromises, right?"

James nodded. She had him there.

"I just want everything to calm down." Shay smiled. "I'll take a month off tomb raids. We can spend time together, walk the dog, and have a lot of steamy, exhausting sex."

James perked up. "Not saying that's a bad thing."

Shay grinned. "Yeah, thought so. I'll have Peyton concentrate on finding lower-level raids to help Lily build up more solo experience in her own name, maybe even a few in the Aletheia name, too." She stood and sauntered toward the hallway. "For now, though, I'm gonna take a shower. After that, I'll give you a little Happy Fun Land experience in the bedroom."

James rose and scooped her up into his arms, and she yelped.

"Save the shower for after," he rumbled.

The woman stared at the screen, frowning as she fast-forwarded through footage of James Brownstone and his bounty-hunter army destroying the Council mutants and wizards who had invaded the amusement park. This whole thing was a waste of her time. She had better things to do than worry about some bounty hunter celebrity. She didn't even know why she'd been sent the footage.

Her eyes widened and she stopped the fast-forward, rewound, and played the footage again at normal speed. Her heart pounded and she swallowed hard as she watched James in his armor form, leaping into the air and firing energy blasts.

"No, no, no. It can't be." She leaned back and placed her hand on her chest, taking deep breaths.

Every damned government on the planet had this footage, and they hadn't done anything to Brownstone. That meant all the programs the Earth governments had developed to prepare them for this very scenario were complete failures.

America's Project Ragnarok, Project Nephilim, and the Fortis group were supposed to be some of the most knowledgeable when it came to extraterrestrial threats, but as far as she could tell, they weren't even looking in Brownstone's direction, assuming he was just another bounty hunter with a nice artifact. The next in line, including the Chinese, British, Indians, Japanese and Russians, didn't care either. The Japanese were even unofficially happy that he'd helped them with the Harriken.

There was only one explanation. They had no idea of the true nature of the creature calling itself James Brownstone, which meant the Earth governments had developed no countermeasures.

How long had the monster been adapting to Earth defenses, or Oriceran defenses for that matter? The famous

Brownstone had fought everyone from gangsters to Drow queens. He might very well be one of the most experienced of his kind ever.

She took several deep breaths and straightened in her chair. It wasn't a time to panic. This was her job, and if the people of Earth didn't know what Brownstone was and hadn't attacked him yet, there was still time. She could surprise him before he reached his true potential.

Her slender hand reached into her desk, and she pulled out a thin silver square. She rubbed the square, and a glowing display appeared, symbols flowing past her ocular implants. Nothing any human could ever hope to understand.

With the help of a few quick visual commands, she initiated transmission mode. It'd been a long time since she had spoken her own language. The words came slowly and haltingly but were clear enough.

"This is Sentry 7921. I will transmit the corroborating data soon, but I hereby report that a Vax Forerunner is present on Earth and operating at least at extended advanced levels. I will shortly be initiating a class-two containment protocol. There is no evidence at this time that any authorities on Earth recognize the threat, and per standing orders, I will handle the matter discreetly and eliminate the Forerunner."

The woman paused the playback, staring at James mid-swing against He Who Hunts. "So you've adapted your strategy, huh? Tested Earth's defenses by pretending to be a bounty hunter?" She narrowed her eyes. "I never thought a Forerunner would be so subtle, but it doesn't matter. I won't let you take this planet no matter what it takes, you Vax monster.

"I swear I'll destroy you, James Brownstone."

FINIS

First, THANK YOU for reading not only this book but these *Author Notes!*

We have embarked on an effort to streamline our production and to do that, I now have to write author notes "days" in advance (well, two weeks) from the book coming out.

I'm kinda afraid of the newness of this.

In my mind, I'm wondering what happens if something goes on between when I write THESE author notes, and the book actually releases? Then I slap myself upside the head and say 'just put the info in the NEXT set of author notes you write.'

That was so obvious, my wife didn't even have to point it out to me.

So, I was talking with a collaborator last week about *The Unbelievable Mr. Brownstone* and how this series must finish. Not with him running into the night never to be seen again – but ready to allow his daughter and her new series to take center stage.

The future is STELLAR!

CHRISTMAS SUCKS... BECAUSE I'M IMPATIENT

So, I'm usually crap at getting presents for Christmas. I'm that last guy in the store, running around frantic, noticing the boxes for the cologne and perfume giveaways have been ripped apart.

When the salespeople notice my eyes, they shy away— not that I blame them. They just had a hella-harsh day, and now, mere seconds before they close, a younger me was coming through the store like a zombie looking for fresh meat.

I just want to apologize to all of those salespeople who have had to deal with me in the past. Also, I'd like to apologize to my family. I know some of those gifts were pretty bad.

The OTHER side of this coin was that when I was a *good* Michael and purchased my gifts at least two weeks ahead of schedule, they didn't suck. When that occurred (hey, stop laughing! It *did* occur!) I would gnaw on my lips, waiting impatiently to give them their gift.

I was like a two-year-old who couldn't stop telling my family to guess what their gift was. I enjoy life just a little bit more now that I don't suffer from this malady nearly so much.

ALL OF THAT TO SAY...

It sucks to know what is coming with the rest of Brownstone, and to not share it with you!

But it is cool. There WILL be one more sacrifice on the team, but you will be ok with it.

I promise.

NEW BOOKS COMING SOON in Oriceran

Be on the lookout for *The Daniel Codex* by Judith Berens – Hitting you October 30, 2018.

Ad Aeternitatem,
Michael Anderle

* Martha Carr and Michael Anderle *

Waking Magic (1) - Release of Magic (2) - Protection of Magic (3) - Rule of Magic (4) - Dealing in Magic (5) - Theft of Magic (6) - Enemies of Magic (7) - Guardians of Magic (8)

The Soul Stone Mage Series

* Sarah Noffke and Martha Carr *

House of Enchanted (1) - The Dark Forest (2) - Mountain of Truth (3) - Land of Terran (4) - New Egypt (5) - Lancothy (6) - Virgo (7)

The Kacy Chronicles

* A.L. Knorr and Martha Carr *

Descendant (1) - Ascendant (2) - Combatant (3) - Transcendent (4)

The Midwest Magic Chronicles

* Flint Maxwell and Martha Carr*

The Midwest Witch (1) - The Midwest Wanderer (2) - The Midwest Whisperer (3) - The Midwest War (4)

The Fairhaven Chronicles

* with S.M. Boyce *

Glow (1) - Shimmer (2) - Ember (3) - Nightfall (4)

CONNECT WITH MICHAEL ANDERLE

Michael Anderle Social
Website:
http://kurtherianbooks.com/

Email List:
http://kurtherianbooks.com/email-list/

Facebook Here:
https://www.facebook.com/OriceranUniverse/
https://www.facebook.com/TheKurtherianGambitBooks/

Printed in Poland
by Amazon Fulfillment
Poland Sp. z o.o., Wrocław

49935149R00167